FLiRT

Close Up and Personal

By Nicole Clarke

GROSSET & DUNLAP
Published by the Penguin Group
Penguin Group (USA) Inc., 375 Hudson Street,
New York, New York 10014, U.S.A.
Penguin Group (Canada), 90 Eglinton Avenue East, Suite
700, Toronto, Ontario, Canada M4P 2Y3
(a division of Pearson Penguin Canada Inc.)
Penguin Books Ltd, 80 Strand, London WC2R 0RL, England
Penguin Ireland, 25 St Stephen's Green, Dublin 2, Ireland
(a division of Penguin Books Ltd)
Penguin Group (Australia), 250 Camberwell Road,
Camberwell, Victoria 3124, Australia
(a division of Pearson Australia Group Pty Ltd)
Penguin Books India Pvt Ltd, 11 Community
Centre, Panchsheel Park, New Delhi - 110 017, India
Penguin Group (NZ), Cnr Airborne and Rosedale Roads,
Albany, Auckland 1310, New Zealand
(a division of Pearson New Zealand Ltd)
Penguin Books (South Africa) (Pty) Ltd, 24 Sturdee
Avenue, Rosebank, Johannesburg 2196, South Africa

Penguin Books Ltd, Registered Offices:
80 Strand, London WC2R 0RL, England

**Cover and interior design by Michelle Martinez Design, Inc.
Illustrations by Marilena Perilli.**

Copyright © 2006 by Grosset & Dunlap. All rights reserved. Published by Grosset & Dunlap, a division of Penguin Young Readers Group, 345 Hudson Street, New York, New York 10014. GROSSET & DUNLAP is a trademark of Penguin Group (USA) Inc. Printed in the U.S.A.

Library of Congress Cataloging-in-Publication Data is available.

ISBN 0-448-44264-7   10 9 8 7 6 5 4 3 2 1

FLiRT

Close Up
and Personal

By Nicole Clarke

Grosset & Dunlap

After two incredible weeks in New York, the strange routine still felt like a cheap shoe. It fit badly and it hurt.

ALEXA VERON—SCHEDULE

1. Try to wake up. Fall back to sleep. Finally get up when my roommate yells at me.
2. Try to eat breakfast way too early. No time for egg-white omelets and low-carb pancakes (*¿qué?*) with the other girls. Grab a croissant with coffee if I'm lucky.
3. Head uptown to the magazine office—block of offices—*city* of offices—to play photographer all day. Spend free time juggling "homework," friends, clubs, and parties.
4. Try to take a picture of my favorite actor of *all time*, who happens to be *in New York* at the same time as me (according to my friend Manuela, who reads all the gossip mags). El Torero—he's like the Spanish James Bond. Only way younger and cuter.
5. Try to make two more meals and curfew. Fail miserably.

Alexa had never had this problem before. Argentines ate dinner late, stayed out late, and knew not to schedule things too tightly in the morning. Here in New York City, she had found, the clubs might stay open till four, but your boss still expected you at work long before any sane person should be up and moving about. And if you had any conscience whatsoever, apparently, you were supposed to spend a healthy amount of time *before* work at the gym and then perfecting your ensemble— not that Alexa did. Breakfast? There just wasn't enough time in the average American day. Ensemble? Fresh, fun, but strictly off the rack. No muss, no fuss.

This morning, Kiyoko had thrown a sandal at her when she didn't respond to the wake-up cursing. Alexa had finally regained consciousness, thrown on some jeans, and dressed them up with a fancy halter top. She tied her long, dark brown hair into a messy bun and grabbed her bag—an oversize Hermès knockoff she'd scored down in Chinatown. Awesome. Hopping out of the loft, she speared a pair of spindly black heels onto her feet.

The others had already left. Alexa didn't like riding the subway by herself, so she took the bus to the Hudson-Bennett building. She barely made it to the cafeteria in time to grab a yogurt and go.

The rest of the *Flirt* interns were getting up from their tables as she waited in line. They were dressed for a day at the office—a *magazine* office, that was—except for Kiyoko, who always dressed for an evening of clubbing and got away with it. Mel and Olivia waved. Gen and Charlotte gave her fake smiles, then arched eyebrows at each other. Kiyoko picked up something from her tray and tossed it at Alexa as she passed.

Alexa caught it. "Hey, *gracias!*"

Kiyoko had saved her a mint. That plus a cup of coffee would round out her breakfast.

"*De nada,* lad. What are roommates for?" Kiyoko wore a green plastic sleeveless minidress today, and tall, black boots on which a red and yellow sun had been painted. She flipped her long, black hair over one shoulder as she walked away.

Alexa grinned, then frowned. Yogurt and a mint. Mami would not approve. Alexa resolved to find some actual from-the-tree fruit—not this weird museum-looking stuff at the register—somewhere today.

Her *Flirt*-issued cell phone beeped. Incoming text message. She paid for her food, sloshed down some black coffee, and paused to read the blurb:

See Ms. Bishop at Flirt first thing this morning. Use the security elevator. Delia.

This was it. The call from Command Central.

Ay, ay, ay! Right now? Time out for some emergency damage control on her hair, at least. "You go on," Alexa called to her friends, who were waiting at the entrance impatiently. "I'll catch up." She turned back toward the restrooms.

Each of the interns would have the chance to prove herself over the course of the eight weeks, and Alexa's turn had come, whether she liked it or not. She had been summoned to the office of Josephine Bishop— fashion icon, social trendsetter, and creator of *Flirt* magazine. Alexa had snapped her picture on impulse at the orientation luncheon two weeks ago. Would Ms. Bishop remember? If so, would she still be pissed off? Well, who knew the woman insisted on left-profile shots only? "It's my good side," she had hissed.

They say you never get a second chance at a first impression, but here it came. *And I have to be wearing jeans,* Alexa thought ruefully. She looked at herself in the wall-size mirror of the ladies' lounge. A sequined, maroon spandex halter top set off her so-faded-they're-almost-white jeans, and she'd tucked a few patterned silk scarves into one back pocket, then pulled them out a bit. In any dance club in the world she would have rocked, but at work, well . . . There wasn't time to go all the way back to the loft and change. She would have to take her chances. Maybe Bishop would think she was being "edgy."

> **" They say you never get a second chance at a first impression, but here it came. "**

Alexa retied her hair and sighed. Life had been so much simpler at home. She hadn't really appreciated that when she accepted this chance-of-a-lifetime internship at the supposedly hottest fashion and beauty magazine in all of New York. Not the pseudo-SoHo or Village *barrios* that had popped up in Buenos Aires. *Nueva York.* *The* New York. Where simple . . . was more complex.

𝕲   𝕲   𝕲   𝕲

This was the way to travel. The mahogany elevator doors whispered shut behind Alexa, and a computer voice asked her to "say or press" her floor number. When she answered, it asked her to "say or press" the first three letters of her last name on the keypad. "V-E-R" was accepted as a valid user, and the elevator moved upward as though it had a personal stake in the outcome of her meeting.

The doors slid open and Alexa stepped out.

"You're late," Delia, Ms. Bishop's secretary, mouthed. She tilted her head at a chair near

Josephine Bishop's door and continued her telephone conversation.

Alexa sat down in the off-white, cushiony chair. She picked up a copy of *Flirt* from the coffee table and leafed through it. After all the hurrying, it was double murder to have to wait. What would she say to Bishop when she got in there, anyway? Every creative idea she'd ever had seemed to have withered and died on the vine.

A male staffer brisked in, dropped off some proofs, and disappeared. The phone lines periodically chuckled, and Delia either curtly took a message or forwarded the call. Alexa paged through the magazine, recognizing some of the models from the gigantic close-up prints that hung on the walls all around her.

Then Delia's intercom made a polite, annoying beep. Though Delia answered via her headset, Alexa could hear the caller through the frosted-glass office door: "Delia! *Where* is that Veron girl?"

"She was a little late, Ms. Bishop."

Alexa glared at Delia for making her wait, then went over and knocked on Bishop's door.

"Hey!" Delia protested.

"Come," called a voice like God's, if God were a woman.

Alexa obeyed the command. She walked through the looking glass and stopped short, suddenly felt very small and insignificant. She found herself in a stretch limo of an office—it seemed to go on forever, with work stations and conversation corners and screened-off areas scattered throughout and, past them, the endless buildings of Manhattan receding behind the huge windows.

Alexa felt a sharp jolt of excitement mixed with fear. This was the real thing! Busy light shone from a board covered with photo negatives. A long couch done up in blue-gray silk dominated one corner. A coffee service was set up on the conference table. Alexa wondered momentarily if the cute coffee guy had delivered it. *Pay attention,* she reminded herself. She was here. Now she had to show that she could handle *being* here.

"Ms. Veron. I'm so glad you've finally found a moment to meet with me this morning." Josephine Bishop sat at a large, glass-topped desk, flipping through a stack of papers. The publisher and CEO looked as though she had put an entire edition of the magazine to bed herself, and it was only eight thirty A.M. She wore a light gray business suit, mostly jacket and barely skirt, along with matching three-inch heels in a buttery-looking leather. She checked her watch and then gazed flatly at

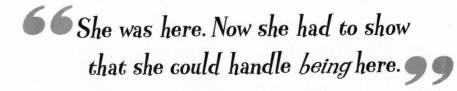

" She was here. Now she had to show that she could handle *being* here. **"**

her intern, not one iota of warmth escaping her eyes or lips. "Delia mentioned you had some medical problem, but the press waits for no one."

Medical problem? What had that slime been telling her boss?

Bishop took in Alexa's outfit, distaste adding to her already splendid mood. "We'll have to talk about your . . . clothes."

"These?"

> ❝ *Medical problem? What had that slime been telling her boss?* ❞

Bishop arched an eyebrow. "Yes."

Denim, Alexa knew, was not considered high couture. Blue jeans were okay for movie premieres and clubbing, but that was about it. According to Olivia, the Fashion department intern, the only time denim showed up on a Paris runway was when some old-fart designer had a midlife crisis. But jeans were what Alexa wore! They were who she was. She'd be taking pictures of models, not vice versa. To a photographer, what was *inside* the designer clothing was of more interest than the labels themselves. She wanted to remind Ms. Bishop that, in the world of fashion design, knowing when to break the rules was the only *real* rule, anyhow. Right?

"Yes, the clothes on your body," Ms. Bishop specified. "This is a place of business. In fact, never

> **To a photographer, what was *inside* the designer clothing was of more interest than the labels themselves.**

mind talking. I want you to see Jonah at The Closet as soon as possible."

Apparently, this wasn't rule-breaking time.

"Now"—Ms. Bishop reached for a file—"let's get to work on our portfolio, shall we? You've had a couple of weeks to think about your topic. Why don't you tell me about your ideas for the photo spread you'll be designing?"

Photo spread! Alexa was still worrying about her jeans. Besides, her artsy concept would never fly at *Flirt*. She needed a fashion angle, but she'd been so busy trying to get to meals, photo shoots, and Lynn Stein's office that she'd completely spaced thinking about the magazine spread. She figured that, under pressure, a worthy idea would just . . . erupt. She hesitated, gazing out the window at the electronic billboards that were visible, advertising Old Navy, a cellular phone service, one of those double-decker bus tours of the city.

> **Photo spread! Alexa was still worrying about her jeans.**

If ever she needed a spontaneous thought, it was now. She opened her mouth, hoping that something dazzling would come spewing out.

"Ms. Veron?"

One of the reader boards showed the front of a tour bus, with its destination lit up.

". . . Central Park," Alexa read, nodding unconvincingly.

The world's most trite, overexposed, washed-out idea for a New York photo essay ever.

"And? . . ."

And what? All she knew about Central Park was that the bad guys had better get out of the way. The new blockbuster *El Torero Unleashed!* had actually been filmed *in Central Park*. The mythic crime/bullfighter El Torero comes back to life to fight gangs in modern-day New York.

Bishop drummed her ice-colored, polished fingers on the desk.

Alexa couldn't come out and say she wanted to lie in wait for El Torero to unleash himself again. She

> ❝*All she knew about Central Park was that the bad guys had better get out of the way.*❞

couldn't admit that she had already been thinking of lurking in leafy patches near the park reservoir, where the movie's climactic scene was filmed—El Torero charging after the entire population of both Bloods and Crips until the two sides finally declared a truce. And she couldn't mention that she and Olivia, who had also seen the film, had agreed to try to re-create that scene using horses from the local riding academy and whichever group of day-camp children might happen to be in the park that day. They'd been kidding, but still.

"Ms. Veron!"

She looked out the window for inspiration again, and down to the street, far below. The only thing that jumped out at her from up here was a white horse and carriage moving along with traffic, a sight that had struck her as incredibly romantic two weeks ago.

She cleared her throat and looked Ms. Bishop straight in the eye. "Central Park and horses! That's it. What I'm interested in are the *styles* of ordinary people in Central Park . . . and, um, horses. I, er, like to infuse urban scenes with natural elements. Man against nature, or man in harmony with nature."

Ms. Bishop gave her a look that acknowledged this as the total bull that it was. But Alexa played it straight.

"Style—it is always changing, no? It is a race, like a horse race, to the finish. Put me up on a horse, with a camera, and I can capture that."

"But Central Park?" Bishop said skeptically.

"Readers will identify with a place that they know, eh? And at the same time, they'll feel the thrill of another world, part of the elite horsey set."

Bishop thought about it. "Horse racing, horse racing . . . The race to fashion. It does have a certain élan," she admitted. "By a long stretch of the imagination. We could tweak it a little, play up the drama. High speed, high stakes, silks and boots—that all says 'sexy.' Could even tie in to the leather issue this fall. 'Central Park, Photo Finish,' " she said, as though she were presenting the idea to Alexa. "Okay, then. Let's give it a shot." She scrutinized her intern a little more deeply. "But are you up to the task? Surely you didn't bring a horse with you." The corners of her lips turned up while her eyes stayed out of it.

"No, but I'm a good rider. Olivia said she leased a horse from the academy that was fine . . ."

"Those glue-factory nags? Heavens no. My interns must, unfortunately, uphold my image. I'll arrange for a more suitable mount for you." She hit a button on her phone and spoke into it. "Delia, get me Grable out in Westchester. And check Jonah's availability." She turned back to Alexa. "I'll have Grable haul someone in. Let's get started. I want you behind a lens in that park every day for the next two weeks. Get a partner. We'll talk to Lynn about a layout." She eyed Alexa's jeans and halter top again. "And for god's sake, ask Jonah for a decent riding kit." She waved a hand as though a lazy, poorly dressed fly had stumbled out of the security elevator.

Alexa turned to leave.

"Oh, and Ms. Veron."

Alexa stopped. "*¿Sí?*"

Ms. Bishop held her motionless with the cold, dead gaze of a shark. "Your reputation is on the line. Don't screw this up."

☙　☙　☙　☙

To: manuelaferguson@sola.net
From: alexa_v@flirt.com
Subject: urban report

Hola, chica,

Sorry I haven't been writing. Everything is fantástico over here so far. How are Fiero and the other ponies? Thanks for taking care of Campo for me. Hey, I might get a chance to ride here in the city! I had a great idea for my photo project involving horses. More on that later.

You know how you always hear bad things about people in New York, but it's like everywhere: half the people are mean, and half the people aren't. Here's the short list:

Doorman: funny, likes futbol—rocks

Ms. Bishop's personal assistant: dead weight, thinks she's all that—isn't

Roommate Kiyoko: Entertainment intern, you'd love how she dresses—rocks

Bishop's niece Gen: Beauty intern, started out sweet, pretends she likes you—doesn't

Her roommate Mel: Editorial intern, American, a good person!—rocks

Gen's identical twin (not really) Charlotte: Fitness intern, only in it for the clothes, thinks she's fooling us—isn't

Olivia: Fashion intern, to-die-for British accent (cuz she is), rides!—rocks

More on the rest of New York (outside the loft) next time, meanwhile, no word yet on El Torero! But thought I saw that chica from the credit card commercial that we like coming out of the Starbucks. Didn't get a pic. Qué lástima!

More news pronto,
Lexa

Everything was not *fantástico,* as Alexa had e-mailed Manuela. She was on probation, in more ways than one. And as she left Bishop's office, Delia had told her that a private car was waiting downstairs to take her to a photo shoot right away. Alexa stood on the curb for twenty minutes before she got a call from Lynn Stein, the photography editor, wondering where in the heck she was and suggesting she get upstairs immediately, or sooner, if possible.

Alexa pictured Delia's perfect-teeth smile of revenge throughout the day, and knew that war had been declared.

She said as much to Kiyoko and Mel, who were hanging out in Alexa's bedroom when she returned to the loft. She stomped in as hard as she dared in the shoes she was wearing and threw herself on her bed.

"So, how'd your interview with Bishop go?" Kiyoko asked evenly from the futon near the window.

Alexa blew a giant sigh. "*Bueno.* But this Delia . . . *She* is the problem. One thing you guys should know about me . . . if there is one thing I hate, it's waiting! I cannot believe this woman—this creature—this *thing*—made me wait for no reason today, twice! And you know why? Because she could. She just told me what to do, and I did it."

"She's on a power trip." Melanie Henderson sprawled on the floor with a non-*Flirt* magazine. "What happened, exactly?"

Alexa recounted the before-and-after scenes at Bishop's office.

"*Sss-t!*" Kiyoko made a sizzling sound. "That burns, lad. Making up the thing about the private car. Making you stand outside when it's ninety degrees. Almost as bad as what she did to me."

"Yeah? What'd she do to you?"

"The wench made me listen to dentist-office music all the way from the airport."

"Whoa," said Mel.

Kiyoko had flown in from Brazil—or was it Dublin? Alexa had lost track. But Alexa knew exactly how she herself had come to be at *Flirt* magazine. It had been a long, tortuous road. And Delia had been the first person she'd met.

❻   ❻   ❻   ❻

What on earth are the odds? Alexa remembered marveling to herself on the flight to New York. How could it happen that such a talented, kind, interesting, beautiful person would nearly get kicked out of high school just when she was looking at colleges? That her parents and her principal would make her apply for a magazine internship to "channel" her "creative energy"? That, out of thousands of candidates, she would actually *get* it? With odds that high and luck that timely, Alexa couldn't say no to two months of taking pictures instead of tests—to a vacation instead of a grounding. Even if the internship was at some stupid American fashion magazine. She'd find a way to make it work for her. This Bishop woman must have seen talent in the photos she'd sent in with her application. Surely, others would, too. Yes, come to think of it, New York would be the perfect place to launch her Big Idea.

The idea had come to her in Rio, while she was on vacation. Her parents, both mathematicians, had taken Alexa and her little sister, Luisa, to a "nerd conference" in Brazil, one of those conventions where university professors spend three days talking about the thrill of numbers. In between sessions, the family played *turista*. As they walked the narrow streets near their hotel one day, a young girl about Luisa's age had jumped out from

66 *With odds that high and luck that timely, Alexa couldn't say no to two months of taking pictures instead of tests.* 99

between two buildings and begged for food. Alexa's father, Dr. Veron, gave her some coins. Alexa's mother, also Dr. Veron, hugged first the child and then speechless Luisa. Alexa clumsily focused the camera she'd received for her birthday from her grandmother and took a picture of the girl's muddy bare ankle. Then she stepped back and captured the full silhouette against a sparkling glass storefront.

The two prints reeked with personality. Alexa sent them in to the *Buenos Aires Herald,* which was holding a photography contest. She beat out who knew how many adults to win first prize: a top-of-the-line Pentax digital camera, a beefy laptop and printer, and all the software and hardware to go with them. *And* her photos made the front page of the newspaper! "Full of truth and depth," read the judges' comments. "Very artistic." Alexa thought the judges had made an excellent choice.

She practiced framing similar shots in every nerd-conference city her family went to: Lima, Caracas, Mexico City. Always portraits, or portions of portraits. This was fun! And maybe there would be money in it, if she could sell her work. For every major city in the world, Alexa knew that tens of thousands of people—maybe millions—wanted to know what it was *really* like to live there. Not just the music, or the smells, or the people, but the feel of the place. And there was only one way to tell it to them straight: with her camera. Because, face it . . . people lied. The lens did not.

When she sent more photographs with her application to the *Flirt* program, Josephine Bishop took one look at them and offered the sixteen-year-old Argentine a summer internship—one of six coveted positions vied for annually by girls all over the world. A few months later, Alexa was en route from her native Buenos Aires to Miami. And from Miami to New York. The plane had circled forever, waiting for its chance to land.

"We are making our final descent into LaGuardia Airport . . ."

Alexa brushed some straggly wisps of hair back from her face and straightened her clothes as best she could. She had finally arrived! It was about time this city got to know Alexa Veron.

As the plane touched down, she pulled her black digital camera out of her bag, pointed it out the airplane window, and snapped a series of frames. She didn't want to miss a moment of this trip. Whatever else might happen during the eight-week internship at *Flirt* magazine, her shutter would be clicking. She planned to get as much footage of the city as possible and sort it all out later. Nothing less than her art was at stake. This would definitely be the start of something huge: New York, Paris, Abu Dhabi! She would travel the globe making art.

But while all of the chosen had arrived at Fashion Central with career hopes, not every girl's immediate high-school fate was riding on the experience as well. Which Alexa Veron's was.

"¡Caramba!" she said under her breath, thinking about it as the plane taxied and taxied. Junior year at Santa Teresa de las Montañas had not begun well. Demerits, suspensions, threats of expulsion . . . Her grades weren't bad, but her "exuberant behavior," as her homeroom teacher put it, bordered on demonic. Yes, she had spray painted the handrails in the stairwells between classes. True, she had switched the hand soap in the restrooms for vegetable oil. It worked so well, she'd tried it on Luisa at home, who promptly cried to Mami. But they had never proven the rest. She kept the photos she took of her victims a secret. The school principal, hoping to focus some of that energy, had *strongly suggested* Alexa apply for the magazine internship at the end of last term. Now that she'd gotten it, Mami, Papi, the nuns,

> 66 *But while all of the chosen had arrived at Fashion Central with career hopes, not every girl's immediate high-school fate was riding on the experience as well.* 99

and even Luisa were all glad to allow her a reprieve *if* she made the internship a success.

But she wasn't going to think about that right now. Maybe not for the whole rest of the trip. Because, on top of the chance to skip school, see the sights, and take pictures for a real magazine, something else had her jumping with nervous energy. It was almost the reason she had applied for the internship in the first place: If her luck held out and the world didn't explode within the next eight weeks, she might catch a glimpse of a certain gorgeous Spanish singer/actor who sometimes

On top of the chance to skip school, see the sights, and take pictures for a real magazine, something else had her jumping with nervous energy.

made New York his home and who, rumor had it, was on the outs with a certain blond American actress. So what if he was a little old for Alexa? He wore his age well. She'd seen him half-naked on a horse in a riveting photo spread in *People en Español*. With a bod sculpted by galloping stallions through the streets of New York and a face embraced by both Madrid and Hollywood, he was so hot, Alexa's blood vessels melted just thinking about him. Her best friend, Manuela, would have a *vaca* if she came home with that photo.

"WELCOME, BIENVENUE, BENVENUTO, BIENVENIDOS A NEW YORK" read part of a sign on the outside of the terminal. "Ha-llo to you, too!" whispered Alexa in her lilting *porteña* accent.

She shuffled off the plane, made her way through customs, and lugged her carry-on bag thousands of kilometers through the terminal, in a daze. When she reached the baggage claim area, she snapped awake, and the bottom of her stomach dropped out.

All of the passengers on her flight looked as though a cheering section were waiting for them . . . except for Alexa. She tried not to let tired tears escape her eyes. Back at the airport in Buenos Aires, her entire family had gathered to see her off—Mami, Papi, Luisa, Nonna, Tío Lolo, Tía Angelita, and a bunch of cousins. Plus Manuela, who broke down and cried. But not a single person had shown up to meet her here.

Unless it was that silent man in the black suit holding a bouquet of red roses and a computer-generated sign that read "A. VERON." The magazine took care of its international guests, though the locals were on their own.

Alexa's mood switched for the third time in ten minutes. *"¡Qué bárbaro!"* she exclaimed. "Totally awesome!"

> *Her beige knit suit shouted "Expensive!" and the toes of her matching pumps ended in points so sharp, they could draw blood.*

Flowers. A chauffeur. A private car. A girl could get used to this.

The man didn't say much, just asked which were her bags as they spun around the conveyor belt. Then he showed her where to wait outside, and moments later, a shiny black Cadillac stopped silently at the curb. The same guy came around and opened the door for her. After traveling all day under her own steam, this was more than welcome. Alexa gave a satisfied smile as she peeked into the backseat.

"You're late," complained a thin, leggy blond woman who nestled in the cushions behind the driver. Her beige knit suit shouted "Expensive!" and the toes of her matching pumps ended in points so sharp, they could draw blood. The tiniest cell phone in the world made her doll-size hands look large, and a compact laptop hid her size-zero lap. "Get in!"

"I wasn't flying the plane, or we would've been here sooner," Alexa joked, sliding onto the seat opposite her. "I'm Alexa Veron. You must be one of the models." She held out a hand to shake.

The woman ignored it. "Models! Think a hundredth of the salary and a hundred times the brain cells." She *tch*ed. "The name's Delia. I'm Ms. Bishop's P.A. Let's go." She motioned to the chauffeur and went back to the cell-phone conversation that Alexa's entrance had interrupted. She clicked away on the computer, murmuring "Mm-hmm" into the phone, apparently paying attention to neither device.

Alexa shrugged and watched out the window as they left the airport behind and drove along in relative silence. Eventually, the highway they were on crossed a river, and they merged onto a downtown street crawling with traffic. Pedestrians choked the intersections. Some buildings were vaguely familiar from American movies and some were like the buildings in every other country Alexa had been to. It was hard to get her bearings.

"*Scusi?* Where are we?" she said out loud, but the glass behind the driver was closed, and no response came from her companion. Alexa felt punchy from the long flight and walk through the airport. After spending hours on her application and beating out thousands of other girls to get here, she had expected to be greeted by

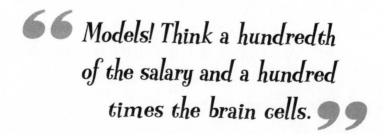

Models! Think a hundredth of the salary and a hundred times the brain cells.

an official from the magazine, if not Josephine Bishop herself. Instead, she was stuck with some brain-dead fashion flunky.

Alexa sighed impatiently. Couldn't the magazine have sent someone more . . . *human* to pick her up? She pulled out her camera at a stoplight and snapped a few shots.

Now Delia deigned to acknowledge her. "You know, you can buy fifty different postcards of that same exact scene at Rite Aid." She snapped her phone shut.

> **" You know, you can buy fifty different postcards of that same exact scene at Rite Aid. "**

Alexa lowered her camera. "Eh?"

"Ms. Bishop has rigorous standards. I hope you've got some ideas that are more *original* for the magazine." Delia flipped down a lighted vanity mirror and patted her immaculate cap of golden hair. She spread her lips to see if anything was stuck in her teeth.

"Oh, I have lots of original ideas," Alexa assured her. "I'm especially interested in natural poses."

"Hardly original," Delia droned, finding a minute celery string or bit of mint floss and attempting to remove it with her little fingernail.

Alexa narrowed her eyes. Delia was asking for it.

"How do you Americans say it? *Dígame queso*," Alexa ordered, raising the viewfinder.

"How's that?" Delia said absently, tugging at the stubborn debris.

"I said: 'Say cheese!' "

Delia stared at her, teeth bared, green thread dangling.

Alexa depressed the shutter.

⊙   ⊙   ⊙   ⊙

And that was how she had ended up in New York City, excused from school, away from her family, and on the loose for two whole months. Check it out: Her plane had touched down just two weeks ago, and already she was working closely with *Flirt* magazine's photography editor, Lynn Stein. Fashion spreads weren't exactly gallery openings, but they might be a high-heeled shoe in the door. If she could keep the demon, Delia, from slamming that door shut in her face.

It turned out that Delia was making a career out of dissing the interns—misscheduled appointments, phantom mandatory meetings . . .

"She's always making little cracks," Alexa complained. "Can you believe she told Bishop I had some sort of medical problem? What's that supposed

> **"You can't always wait around for karma to do its job. Some people have to get what they deserve."**

to mean?"

"She even stole my shoes one day!" Mel said. "I swear they were under my desk. I had to walk barefoot to The Closet and beg a pair from Jonah."

"I'm not saying she deserves life in prison," Kiyoko went on. "I'm just saying there must be something we can do to get back at her."

Alexa grinned. "Torture?"

"Sure, but what kind?"

"It depends. Mental or physical?"

"Let's go with mental. Hurts just as much, leaves less scar tissue."

"You two are sick," said Mel.

"Sorry, earth girl," Kiyoko said. "You can't always wait around for karma to do its job. Some people have to get what they deserve." She looked at Alexa. "That ride from the airport must have been a gross-out, what with Delia scraping things out of her mouth. You say you have evidence?"

"*Sí.* I have a terrible photo of her."

"We could add a link to my website."

Appreciation dawned in Alexa's big, dark brown

eyes. "You mean blog it?" Kiyoko Katsuda was becoming her fast friend for making such bold suggestions time and again. Clearly, *Flirt*'s Entertainment intern could be counted upon to instigate . . . whatever needed instigating. "You would do very well at my Catholic high school," Alexa murmured. "But what happens when she finds out?"

"Who's going to find out?"

They both looked at Mel.

"You're not going to tell, are you?" Kiyoko's big-sister-on-too-much-caffeine tone would have easily cowed Luisa, Alexa was sure. It seemed to work on Americans, too.

"I'm not a narc," Mel retorted. "But what goes around comes around." She smiled, taking the edge out of her words.

"Deep," said Kiyoko.

Alexa felt a little rush. She had always kept her incriminating photos secret. This would be—different. She'd be published again, that's what mattered. A blog might be just one page in a limitless sea of websites, but that was okay. Not in-your-face, not overly obvious . . . In fact, it would almost be their own little secret . . . but that would be enough.

"*Bueno.*"

"Let's use your laptop, lad," Kiyoko said. "I'll key you in as a user on my account, and you can add to the blog whenever. My gift to you. It can be your own visual journal of *Flirt*-ness."

"Plus all the stars I am going to take pictures of as soon as I see them."

Mel folded her arms. "And the bars of the jail cell you'll be getting familiar with when you're arrested for stalking and defaming the celebrity elite."

"Zip it, Melvin. The Internet is a freedom-of-speech zone. You should be all for that."

Kiyoko finished typing and passed the computer to Alexa.

"It's not like she's naked or anything." Alexa scrolled through her folders to find the photo of Delia. A few clicks from her mouse, and Delia's teeth moved right into the template—one close-up and one full portrait of her shocked facial expression.

> **It's not like she's naked or anything.**

"*¡Muy de la banana!*" Alexa proclaimed.

"What's that?"

"It means *excelente, chica!*"

"*Muy de la banana.* I like that." Kiyoko reached over and stuck an empty cartoon balloon next to Delia's open mouth.

Alexa chuckled. "This could be fun. What should the caption say?"

> **Despite her looks, talent, and endless good luck, her good-natured manner made it hard to resent her.**

"Dunno, lad. I don't write words. Just music." Kiyoko tilted her head. "And no words can do my music justice."

"What on earth do you play?" Mel piped up. "The didgeridoo?"

Kiyoko glared at her. "Ha ha. I don't play anything. I do it all on computer."

"That's creative," Mel said drily. She was teasing. Mel adored Kiyoko, and, well, everyone adored Mel. Despite her looks, talent, and endless good luck, her good-natured manner made it hard to resent her. So Kiyoko would sometimes pretend.

"You're so smart, earth girl, what do *you* think the caption should be?"

Melanie's reporter instinct overrode her personal ethics. She got up off the floor and leaned over Alexa's computer screen. "Well . . . as an objective observer . . ." She scrutinized the grimace on Ms. Bishop's personal assistant, caught in the act of overt hygiene maintenance. Then she picked up the mouse and blacked out a couple of teeth. "How about: 'The "Seafood" Diet—Manhattan's hottest new trend'? Get it?"

Kiyoko slid her an amused glance.

Alexa laughed and pointed at the screen. *"Muy de la banana,"* she said.

chapter three

A while later, a knock came at their bedroom door.

"*Pásale,*" called Alexa from her bed.

"*Entrez-vous,*" said Kiyoko, who now perched on the edge of the futon, painting her nails with Wite-Out.

Mel was in a yoga pose on the floor. "Come on in."

The door opened to reveal the only male resident of the loft. His handsome, tan face was framed by shaggy brown hair and punctuated by two lively eyes the color of his jeans. His smile seemed to hold some special secret. A dusty-brown T-shirt in a nubby fabric climbed up his torso, showing off his taut navel area. *Can a belly button have muscles?* Alexa wondered. The boy's lean, tan arms flexed as he braced against the door jamb.

"Hi, Nick," Melanie said sweetly. Why she was going for the one off-limits guy in all of New York City, Alexa didn't know. Alexa herself wouldn't think twice about flirting with any cute *papi,* even if he had a woman—but only if that woman *wasn't* his mother and *wasn't* the house adviser assigned to watch over her 24/7 for two months. Which Nick's was. And anyway, he had a girlfriend, too. So, never mind.

"Hey, ladies," Nick gallantly addressed all of them. "Pizza's here. House meeting, downstairs, five minutes."

> **66 Do you believe him coming on to me like that? 99**

They had been through this twice before.

"Tell Mommy we'll be there," Kiyoko said, and Nick's smile froze. Then he pushed away from the door and was gone. "Do you believe him coming on to me like that?"

Alexa shrugged. Kiyoko *always* thought guys were hitting on her. Of course, she was usually right.

"If Matteo were here, he'd kick Nick's butt. But last I heard, he was in Istanbul." She sighed, probably thinking of her super-adorable, super-long-distance boyfriend, and went back to working on her nails.

Alexa grabbed her camera, and Melanie found a notebook and pencil. The two of them ran into Charlotte on her way downstairs to the great room. The curly-haired intern complained loudly to no one in particular, "Do we have to do these meetings every week?"

"I hope not," Alexa said. "Meetings mean rules."

"Who cares?" said Mel, skipping past them and down the stairs. "There's pizza!"

"There had better be cheeseless slices this week," Charlotte pouted.

They drifted into the great room, where Olivia stood talking with Emma Lyric, the house mom as well as Nick's. Emma wore a dress that looked like a couch but was probably as comfy. Olivia, in imported riding breeches and tall black boots, appeared to have just come in from her afternoon hack. This made Alexa miss Campo, the horse she rode on her grandmother's *estancia*.

Mel took one end of the big, red U-shaped couch. Alexa pulled two pillows from a jumble of throws and settled with them onto the floor.

"I love your jeans, Alexa," Charlotte purred, seating herself primly on one of the suede-covered futons. "They almost look used. Where'd you get them?" Her immaculate velour Lacoste tank dress had either never been worn or had been dry-cleaned.

"Yes, where?" echoed Gen as she descended the spiral staircase and joined her friend. "They're so . . . vintage chic." The petite brunette's creased $250 jeans magnified the insult. Genevieve Bishop preferred aged Citizens of Humanitys to ripped Levi's. She claimed that the hand-painted purple scarf she wore with them had been a gift from Madonna. She sat down and crossed her bare ankles to show off her new Gucci sandals.

Alexa ignored her. "You like?" she said to

66 *I love your jeans, Alexa. They almost look used. Where'd you get them?* 99

Charlotte, as though they were having a conversation. "I've worn these pants for three years. I can still fit into them."

Gen looked her up and down. *"Really?"*

"That's so cool!" Mel said, causing Gen, with whom she shared a room, to give her the same look. "By making your clothes last longer, you're saving, like, tons of resources. Cotton is a very demanding crop. Next time, go for hemp pants. More earth-friendly."

"It's called fashion, granola girl," Kiyoko said, appearing just as their five-minute warning expired and stretching out opposite Mel on the couch as if it were a chaise lounge. She had changed into a purplish denim miniskirt, riveted with silver studs. She kicked off her yellow rubber platform sandals, which clunked heavily on the hardwood floor.

"It's not the jeans but how they're worn," put in Olivia, who had broken off her conversation with Emma when Gen came in. She took a seat in the middle of the couch and smoothed her white breeches. "Show them, Alexa." Alexa obliged by jumping up and turning a circle. "See the silk scarves, worn just so? The sequined halter? They quite represent the look that's coming out of Argentina right now. On the downscale side." Olivia's knowledge of the scene had earned her a fashion internship; the Bourne-Cecils always made the invitation list at the Paris shows.

"They're cute jeans, but they are kind of trashed," said Gen, now that someone else had said so. "Why don't you toss them and come shopping with us tomorrow?"

"These are my babies!" Alexa said, shocked at the idea.

"Toss them!" Mel said, just as shocked. "Reduce, reuse, recycle. Take them to the Goodwill, if anything." Mel's idea of fashion was about seven layers of tank tops, a huge prairie skirt, and flip-flops. She'd completely captured the whole "Dumpster-chic" look—totally by accident.

"Right," Gen agreed. "Then with the money you get, you can go shopping with us!"

There was a moment of uncomprehending silence.

Then Mel clarified, "You don't *sell* stuff to the Goodwill, Gen; you *donate* it."

Kiyoko snickered. "Probably never even been to one."

"Said the queen of all thrift stores," Gen said.

"Hey, when it works, it works."

❝ Mel's idea of fashion was about seven layers of tank tops, a huge prairie skirt, and flip-flops. ❞

"What is this Good Will?" Alexa asked.

"Yes? What are you talking about?" Olivia looked utterly clueless.

Kiyoko picked up one of her yellow platform sandals. "Where you find this kind of stuff. You know, like at the charity shops in London. Slummin' at the Goodwill."

"Did someone say Goodwill?" Emma breezed back in from the kitchen and set several flat white boxes on the dining table. She picked up the hem of her skirt. "I got this dress there."

"I can see that," said Gen, with fake earnestness.

Emma shot her a glance.

"But 'recycled' is in right now," she added hastily. "Melanie was just telling us." As house adviser, Emma was the law in the loft, and even Genevieve Bishop had to abide by the rules or pack her Louis Vuittons.

"Let's eat!" said Emma, changing the subject. "Nick!" she called.

In a replay of the last two weeks, he came in from the kitchen with a stack of napkins and paper plates, and started opening pizza boxes. Alexa followed the movements of his strong,

It was okay, she told herself, to like parts of Nick Lyric.

brown fingers. She noticed Melanie doing the same. Hey. It was okay, she told herself, to like *parts* of Nick Lyric.

He identified which pies had which toppings, and the girls lined up to help themselves—except for Gen Bishop, who sat on the futon, tapping her foot until Charlotte brought her a slice (cheeseless, of course) and a cup of diet soda.

While Alexa had at first been relieved that pizza existed in this country, now she craved the kind made by her favorite pizzeria back home. There were lots of Italians in B.A., including her grandmother, who was half Italian. "Can't you order a steak pizza?" she asked Emma, who laughed. "Yeah!" Kiyoko cheered. Melanie gave a howl and shouted, "Gross!"

Mel was a militant vegetarian. She had written a big exposé on animal testing at a cosmetics company for her internship project. Giving up lipstick was one thing, but giving up meat? Alexa shook her head as she served herself a pepperoni, sausage, and ground beef wedge. That would be an impossible habit to break. As far as she knew, no one in her country had ever tried it.

Gen picked the toppings off the crust and forked them into her mouth bit by bit. Charlotte did the same. They tried to preserve their lipstick by chewing with their lips pulled back, but the gooey sauce dripped from the corners of their mouths.

Olivia raised her eyebrows and made a napkin-wiping gesture, and they dabbed at their lips, making them worse than ever. They looked like vampires.

Alexa set her plate down, hit the power on her camera, focused, and flashed it at them.

"Heyyy!" came the chorus, which only allowed for further drippage.

Alexa quickly panned the room, taking a few more pictures as cover, ending with one of Emma helping herself to another slice. "We should have pictures from every meeting," she said, as though she really valued these chances to gather and discuss house rules.

When they'd finished, Nick cleared away the plates and boxes, and his mother called the meeting to order. Emma Lyric could move from good-natured pal to disciplinarian in a heartbeat. "It has come to my attention that someone has been messing with the lightbulbs." The girls exchanged innocent, concerned nods. "Now, you know who you are . . ."

Alexa lowered her eyebrows in what she hoped was an accusing scowl. People had been hitting buttons or flipping switches to no avail. It was getting annoying.

Emma shook her head. "I replaced half a dozen bulbs before I realized they weren't burned out, just loosened. And these aren't cheap bulbs. Nick and I have been crawling all over this place screwing them in. That's not what I'm getting paid for, and I want it to stop."

"Yeah," Charlotte agreed.

It was an old trick, but a good one. Alexa had gotten away with that one for months at school. She'd quit before anyone caught on.

> **It was an old trick, but a good one.**

"Now, regarding schedules," Emma continued, "most of you are getting with the program, but as a reminder: We do have to answer to your parents or guardians. Please be punctual to evening meals or let us know ahead of time if you aren't going to make it."

Alexa was used to sitting down to dinner at home around the time loft curfew kicked in. She waved an arm. "But how do we know ahead of time if we're going to be late?"

Emma regarded her. "In your case, Alexa, I think it's a given." Some of the girls laughed. "The only reason you managed it today was because I used bait."

Alexa thought back, picturing Nick's lean body in the door frame. She grinned. "He *is* kind of cute."

> **He is kind of cute.**

Emma sat up straight. "I was talking about the pizza!"

"Uh, yeah," Alexa mumbled, sliding a glance at Mel, whose eyes widened. "Me too."

Emma reminded everyone that curfew was eleven o'clock during the week, twelve on weekends, "but I'm sure you'll *all* remember that."

She eyed Kiyoko, who had come in after midnight the night before, saying she'd lost her watch. She must have found it, because now she made a show of checking her wrist as if to prove to Emma how conscientious she was going to be.

After the meeting broke up, Alexa caught Olivia still resting on the couch. "Hard ride today?" she asked, wanting to know if the clothes were just for show, or what.

"How did you—?" Olivia glanced at her clothing and gave a quick, sheepish grin. "Oh, right! The outfit. Yes, I finally found the academy and went for a ride. It had been a while. I haven't had the time to train, what with getting ready for this trip and all. You've mentioned that you like to ride. Do you keep horses?"

Alexa sat down next to her. "I wish. We can't keep them in the city. Both my parents teach at the *universidad,* and there's no time . . . But on weekends, me and my friend Manuela ride out on my grandmother's place in the country." She reached into her back pocket and pulled out a crumpled photograph. "This is my horse, Campo. He's got an awesome canter."

Olivia nodded approvingly.

"What about you?"

"I'm down to two horses right now, both Dutch Warmbloods. This little gelding I leased down at the academy seemed small to me, but he was fine for a trot through Central Park. You have to ride a couple of blocks in traffic to get there, but the bridle path is a lovely go-round. Why don't you come out with me and Jason sometime?"

"Who's Jason?"

"The school horse, of course."

Alexa smiled mysteriously. "I think I can do better than that." She would need an assistant. "How would you like to help me with my assignment?"

"This involves riding?"

Alexa nodded. "Oh, yes."

"Might it involve the leading man from *El Torero Unleashed!*?"

"*Posible.*"

Olivia looked intrigued. "Love to."

chapter four

It was going to be a triple-latte day. Alexa had started rating each morning by the response she got from the cute coffee guy as she hurried past Café Adèsso.

The first day she noticed him, he looked up from the order he was putting together and smiled at her. Alexa glanced over her shoulder, in case the smile was meant for someone else. But all of the *Flirt* girls had moved on, and a toothless old man in a raincoat crept along the mezzanine behind her. She returned the coffee guy's smile. His curly, light brown hair ebbed around his face and flowed over his collar. Muscled arms stuck out of a white T-shirt. A black apron and jeans hid the rest of him. But the legs were long, Alexa saw, and . . . *I wonder, what color are his eyes?* Late, as usual, she had forced herself to keep moving.

Today, he had not only smiled but waved. If he ever actually spoke to her, she would just have to douse herself in espresso and milk and be done with it. Alexa was hurrying already because Delia had told her to check in with Jonah first thing. Coincidence? Or sabotage?

She found her way to The Closet, but it was locked. *¡Qué lástima!* Her dormant fashion instincts came alive in the face of free clothes, and she could really do some damage here. But one man held the golden key card. Alexa moved a stack of magazines and sat down on the hard, metal chair in the corridor to wait for him.

Beautiful people passed up and down the hall, absorbed in being absorbed in something. Techno music pounded from a hidden speaker, and a burned smell wafted from a nearby break room. Pulsing telephones and laughter and urgent voices all swirled together, none of them requiring Alexa's attention. She picked at a scab on her elbow, wondering what this little adventure would bring. Maybe she could prop the door open for a later, unscheduled visit . . .

She heard Jonah Jones approaching before she caught sight of him.

"Clear the area!" came a high-pitched yet commanding male voice. "The shortest distance between two points is my boot to your butt. This means you!" Several thuds suggested some poor staffer scrambling out of the way.

The ankle boot in question came around the corner first, followed by its mate—side zips in red calfskin, topped by striped flood pants that clung to every adjacent body part and a white, mesh muscle tee. The fair-skinned man sported red-framed glasses, short, spiky blond hair, and a tattoo of an angel on his forearm. Alexa rose to meet him.

"Everyone I know is dying to get out of the

closet—you want in. Alexa, darling. Welcome back." He unlocked the door and let her in.

The interns had been introduced to The Closet's treasure trove of designer samples during their first week, and Jonah Jones was its famous and infamous keeper. The sought-after fashion stylist also hosted a sympathetic "worst-dressed" show on cable TV, and he could be found on just about any red carpet with cameras in front of it, airing his "wish-I-could-be-tactful-but" opinion on the celebs' outfits.

Alexa raised her camera and gave him a questioning look. He graciously mugged several poses for Alexa's camera, without ever worrying about which side of his profile she was capturing. Finally, they got down to business.

"So, tell me. What do the gods have in store for us today? Shoes? Party dress? Lingerie?" Jonah asked.

"I wish. But nothing like that."

Jonah stood back to assess her. His baby blue eyes narrowed as he took in her outfit. "Is. That. The. BCBG? The one I gave you?" The question ended in a sharp squeak.

"Um, sort of." Alexa couldn't deny it; she knew he knew, anyway. Jonah *had* given it to her one day. He had gushed that the stylish little BCBG halter dress with the skirt of silk scarves was absolutely made for her. And perhaps it was: Alexa had used bits of it in several different outfits since then. Well, she was planning to put it all back together at some point. Right now, what remained were about half of the original scarves and a few rows of sequins on the multihued top. She had layered the dress over a filmy, black full slip.

Jonah twirled an index finger. "Spin," he ordered.

Slowly, Alexa turned a circle.

"Autrement."

She spun the other way.

For a moment he said nothing, appraising her. Then he drew near and showered her with air kisses. "It works! You're a secondhand genius!" He lowered his voice. "Just don't mention this to the powers that be . . ." He escorted her toward the racks, pausing at lingerie. "Now, fair maiden. Shall we fit you with a corset? Petticoat? Bustier?"

Alexa smiled. "More like breeches, boots, hard hat. I'm working on a 'Central Park from horseback' theme. Ms. Bishop sent me for some riding clothes."

"Well, why didn't you say so!" Jonah said good-naturedly. "Walk this way." He brisked down the aisle, tucking in a sleeve here or a hem there. They crossed about half an indoor city block to the sporting wear

> **"It works! You're a secondhand genius!"**

section, which Alexa hadn't seen before. The racks bloomed with high-tech apparel for every imaginable sport. Ski suits, tennis garb, gym wear. Visors, helmets, headbands. Cleats, court shoes, Top-Siders.

Then Alexa saw the riding clothes. Velvet caps and shining tall boots, leather gaiters and impeccably styled breeches. Western hats and chaps and pointy-toed boots in every shade of the rainbow, with or without rhinestones and feather accents. But none of the casual loose pants and neckerchiefs of the gaucho; she'd have to suggest those. She was about to mention this hole in the inventory when Jonah stopped short and reached for a hanger. He held up a Sunkist-orange Western show suit and matching hat in front of his own clothes and above his head and primped.

Alexa pictured him on a white horse with flowers in its mane and laughed. "Rodeo queen?" she quipped.

"Cowboy drag," he deadpanned. "Can you imagine?" He replaced the clothing and riffled through some English wear. "You're what, about a twenty-six tall? Let's see, let's see. Jodhpurs? Or breeches?" He studied first the pants, then Alexa. Certainty blinked in his eyes. "With those legs? Jods." He snatched several more items from the shelves. "Hunt coat, gloves, paddock boots." The navy coat appeared to be cashmere, the buff gloves an elegant crochet stitch, and the chic, black ankle boots could have found a home on any dance floor.

Alexa had her eye on some tall boots in gleaming English leather. She had always wanted a pair. She reached out and touched them reverently.

"No, dear, no!" Jonah admonished her. "Tall boots in July? You'll swelter, and they'll only hide your legs. Take my word for it. Try these on." He handed her a bundle of clothes and gear and shunted her off toward a fitting room.

When she emerged, Jonah stood talking to a gaggle of female models. "All right, all right. Borrow away, and then off to your party. But just this once," he cautioned. "Do it quick, and get out of here! You'll draw more of you, like flies."

One of them chose a double-breasted pinstripy thing from a nearby rack, causing Jonah to flatten a hand on his chest. "What is this, the eighties? I don't think so! It's Joe Montana with a sex change. Lose the shoulder pads, my pet."

The others vied for his opinion, but, sensing Alexa's presence, he turned his attention on her. She stood nearly as tall as the models, who all stared at her, too. She was something out of a *telenovela,* the imperious soap opera wife of some rich cattle baron, whom all the women despised but the ranch hands wanted to . . . not despise.

Jonah's brows went down, and his chin came up. He blocked off his view of Alexa's face with both hands, clucking, and then spoke as if to himself. "Beautiful cut on those high waists, so Euro. I like the unsubtle red of the shirt—try it with a black sports bra. And of course, the jacket's just to sling over one shoulder in this heat. It all brings to mind a young Grace Kelly, Liz Taylor, Caroline Kennedy." He dropped his arms and took a critical look at Alexa's hair, then frowned. "Body, yes. Hair, no."

Her hands went to her mass of hair and clips and combs on top of her head. "What's wrong with it?"

Jonah tossed some of his famous empathy her way. "Nothing, hon. And everything."

He clapped his hands sharply to break up the group of browsers. "Girls! Girls! Follow me. Come see the magic happen!" He grabbed Alexa by the hand and pulled her toward a back staircase and down a maze of hallways to a corner of the beauty department she'd never seen before. He plunked her down in a chair in the makeshift salon. Mirrors faced every which way among hair dryers and trays of tools. The blended scent of fifty different hair products hung in the air. Jonah checked his see-through watch. "I've got a thing in twenty minutes! I just want to show you how to put your hair up properly. Now, watch how I do it."

He pulled over a little rickety cart on wheels as though he were leading a poodle on a leash. He fished through several drawers, found the bottle he was looking for, and set out several implements with the precision of a surgeon. Then he reached for Alexa's hair, undid the mess, and shook it out. He met Alexa's eyes in one of the big, round mirrors on the wall. "You have lovely hair, kitten. There's just one rule." He held up a straightening iron in one hand and a scissors in the other. "Use it or lose it."

Alexa had been growing her hair since the third grade. "Okay, okay! I'll use it, *te prometo*. Show me what to do."

"So be it." He plugged in the iron.

Seven minutes later, Alexa's hair shone in a classic French twist. Jonah gave her a hand mirror so she could see it from all sides. Whatever Jonah had massaged into it had worked; the kinks lay flat and shining. The burgundy streaks he had painted in were dazzling against her skin and the collar of the red show shirt. A simple, matching lipstick outlined her lips.

Wow, Alexa thought. *Same hair, world of difference.*

The group of models peeked askance in the mirrors at their own hair, no longer satisfied. One tried to beg a treatment, but Jonah quieted her. "I must be off. But first!" He ripped the silver smock from Alexa's neck and drew her over to a full-length mirror.

A polished young lady looked back at them, resplendent in formfitting deerskin riding pants, trendy black boots, and sheer red shirt. She let the navy cashmere coat dangle carelessly from one finger. This was as close to perfection as Alexa had ever come. *¡Qué bonita!* Manuela wouldn't even recognize her!

Jonah kissed his fingers and sent the gesture heavenward. "Stupendulous! Marvelescent! *Fantastique!* If I do say so myself." He caught Alexa's eye. "How do you like it?"

Alexa turned to admire all her angles in the mirror, first this way, then that. She fingered the rich fabrics and noted the shine on her boots. If she looked this good here, she knew she would look fabulous on a horse. But something was missing. She cocked her head. "Maybe some accessories?" she suggested.

Jonah put a hand to his chin. "One second." He dashed away.

He returned a few minutes later with a black leather riding crop. "From my personal stash," he said, handing it to Alexa.

She took the whip and struck a pose. The models exchanged jealous glances in the mirror.

Jonah regarded her with pride. "How about now, *señorita*?"

They all looked in the mirror.

Alexa stared back, gorgeous. "As we say back home, *muy de la banana*."

Jonah nodded enthusiastically. *"Muy,"* he agreed.

Next stop, photo department. Alexa arrived to find Lynn Stein clicking on a computer at the desk in her office. Her curly red hair poofed out from her head, and glasses with wide, green plastic frames slipped down her nose as she worked. She pressed a button on the wireless headset she wore and spoke into it. "Note to self: Don't forget to try a close-up from the Brooklyn." She noticed her protégée and grinned. "Easier than losing a bunch of Post-its off a bridge," she explained.

"Hi, Lynn. You beeped?"

"One second." She finished typing something, then pushed away from her machine, got up, and led Alexa over to a low couch near the window. The Manhattan melting pot bubbled away a dozen stories below. "Let's take a meeting. Ms. B. wants you on task, pronto. Never mind that I am swamped and up to my eyeballs in this issue." She noticed Alexa's new clothes. "Wow, Jonah must be on another Kentucky Derby kick. Looks great."

Flirt's photography editor reminded Alexa of a dandelion. Her sunny personality hid deep, tenacious roots. Once she made up her mind on a certain shoot, no one—not city bureaucrats or celebrities or even Ms. Bishop—could stop her. They never even knew they were being manipulated. She could make people see things her way, a valuable skill in a photographer. Pit her against another dandelion type, though, and the fluff could fly.

"Now, tell me about this photo essay. How many cameras will we need? We're overbooked right now. We'll have to think about lighting, and I'll get someone working on permits . . ."

Alexa put up a hand. "We don't need all that."

A wise look came over Lynn's petite face. "Hon, it's difficult, but it can be done. Ms. B. said Central Park, and that's no walk in the park. No pun intended. Throw animals into the mix and it's a logistical nightmare. And right when we're in the middle of this 'Survivor: The Models' thing . . ."

"Eh?"

"You know the show *Survivor*. Do you know anything about models? Well, we're getting the three biggest supermodels in the world all together in one place, as part of the teams. Megamodels. So mega they only go by their first initials: I., H., and C. And they wouldn't even use those if they didn't have to have something for a monogram. They're so damned mega they've never been filmed together before, and we're putting them on an island with a camera crew . . ."

"That's awesome!"

"Well, I say that. We haven't got them *yet*. That's the problem. If one can make the shoot, the others

66 We won't need a crew because I'm the one doing the camera work. 99

can't. If two are available, the other one's off in Borneo for three weeks. Then there's the money . . . We've got people working on it."

"You'll get them," Alexa said.

Determination bloomed in Lynn's face. "We will," she vowed. "It's good for the magazine. But what's up with you?"

"Well, we won't need a crew because I'm the one doing the camera work," Alexa explained. "From horseback."

Lynn's eyebrows shot up. "From on top of a horse?"

Alexa nodded, the project taking shape as she thought about it. "It'll be all digital, and natural light."

"And your focus . . . ?"

"Spontaneous fashion. At least, that's what Ms. Bishop seemed to be interested in. That, and bringing the horsey theme into the city. The race to fashion, something like that."

Lynn considered this. "So, the normal weird sights from a new angle. Not that that hasn't been done, but a horse really is a new angle. Those suckers are big." Lynn herself barely hit five feet tall. "What about an assistant? Who'll keep track of shots, memory, time?"

Good thing Alexa had already asked Olivia. Working together, they'd be free to get the candid shots she wanted . . . and to make sure they'd have El Torero all to themselves, if he ever did appear.

"Um, voice recorder. Like you have. And Olivia— she's the Fashion intern—wants to ride with me. She's asking Demetria for some time off. We won't need anybody else. We should be safe enough in the park on horses."

"Sounds good. If you think you can do all that, I'm with you. Make sure I have daily updates on your whereabouts. We'll pick a time to huddle, look at proofs, try to build a theme. That'll keep you on track and me free to worry about the three tenors." She grinned. "Oh, and one more question."

"Yeah?"

"You didn't bring a horse with you from Argentina, did you?"

"As a matter of fact, I did." Alexa reached into her black leather minibackpack, which Jonah had added to her wardrobe along with extra shirts and jods. "This is Campo." Alexa showed her mentor the photograph of her grandmother's stocky black horse. "I've ridden him since I was six."

"He's beautiful," Lynn said with admiration.

"He is. And he's a clown." Alexa stuffed the picture back in her bag.

Lynn's phone rang, and she spoke into her wireless headset. "Stein." She lowered her voice. "Yes, Ms. Bishop." She listened for a moment. "To the street. I certainly will." She paused. "For a horse trailer? Gotcha."

She hung up. "I love this job." She got up from the sofa and motioned for Alexa to follow her.

They brisked through the halls, took the elevator down two floors, and marched along another hallway. "Let's just stop and give Trey a heads-up," Lynn said over her shoulder as her key card let them into Editorial. Frantic pop music scurried through hidden speakers. Smartly dressed lackeys ran copy between offices while the important people hovered behind glass walls with wooden blinds.

Lynn and Alexa passed through an unsecured door and the music changed. Was there a rave this afternoon? Techno dance-grind bounced off the walls. Alexa loved it. Too bad she didn't get the Entertainment beat.

"*S-nap*, lad!" Kiyoko greeted Alexa from a corner of the dividerless room. She was playing receptionist for her mentor, Trey. "What brings you to the good side of town?"

"Getting my photo shoot together. I guess you

guys are going to find space for it?"

"Bossa nova! First I've heard, though."

"Trey?" Lynn asked, cutting to the chase.

Kiyoko hit the page button on the desk phone. "Mr. Narkisian, Mr. Narkisian, please pick up the white courtesy telephone. Your party is waiting for you. Your car lights are on. Your house is burning down. Your mother is on the phone." She looked at Lynn. "That usually gets him."

"Brilliant."

Kiyoko signed on for the Central Park project immediately: "It's either that or cover some stupid grade-school rock band this week. Not exactly my target market. So what do we have to do?" Kiyoko asked.

Lynn stepped in. "You find some way to tie 'Central Park, Equestrian Style' into Leisure, or wherever else you can fit it, and you come up with a sensational layout for National Velvet here." She nodded at Alexa as *Flirt*'s Entertainment editor strode up to the conversation pit that acted as a waiting room. He looked to be about thirty or forty—Alexa never could tell age in old people— but he still looked good. With his wavy, streaked brown hair, good cheekbones, and perfect tan, Trey Narkisian had metrosexual written all over him.

"How are you? Hope I didn't keep you." Trey barely glanced at the new and improved Alexa. His steel-colored eyes pointed out the window, following a migration of models through the skyway between the cluster of buildings. No mortal woman even bothered to hope. It would be too distracting having to work with him. Luckily, Kiyoko had her own boyfriend to think about. Wherever he was.

"Trey, we're here about Alexa's project," Lynn said pointedly, snapping him back to real time.

"Oh, sure," he said vaguely.

"She's going to collab with your department on a photo essay. We should all meet this time Wednesday and hammer out the space considerations. Okay?"

"Right."

"And don't forget our little you-know later."

Are the two editors getting it on? Alexa wondered.

"I won't," he said, his eyes drifting toward the window again.

Lynn cleared her throat.

"I *won't*," he repeated.

She waited for him to go back to work at his drafting table before ushering Alexa out.

They descended in the peon elevator and crossed the wide lobby. "I have to get right back upstairs," Lynn said, "so I'll be leaving you with Ms. Bishop's driver. She said to look for a horse trailer . . ."

They circled through the automatic revolving doors and into the courtyard. There it was, parked in the half-moon driveway. The horse world's poshest rig: a gleaming two-horse trailer, pulled by a spotless, block-long pickup truck. Both vehicles were black, trimmed in gold-painted filigree, and both bore small, tasteful lettering that read "BISHOP THOROUGHBREDS, BEDFORD, NEW YORK."

The driver, dressed in black coveralls with "Hal" embroidered on them, opened the rear door of the king cab, and Alexa got in. They pulled away and crawled through the Midtown streets toward the Upper West Side. After a few difficult turns with the trailer, they stopped in front of the riding academy that Olivia had mentioned. The stately, tan brick building with arched windows and doorways looked more like a posh hotel than a glorified barn. It was several stories tall.

"Ms. Bishop has arranged to lodge the animals here temporarily," said Hal. He let her out of the backseat and went around to the back of the trailer. Alexa watched him open the door, unclip a bungee, and back a dark brown horse out, right into the street. There wasn't exactly a pasture in the middle of Manhattan. "This is Harvard," he said. "He's primarily a hunter/jumper, though he ran a few races as a youngster. He's steady as a rock, and Ms. Bishop recommended him for you."

"Hello, Harvard," Alexa said softly. She held out a closed fist for the animal to sniff, and Harvard gave her a gentle snuffle. The horse wore shipping bandages and boots, a head bumper, and a black sheet with gold trim. Alexa could tell there was some serious horseflesh underneath, and a little knot of excitement grew in her stomach.

Someone from the academy came to the curb to collect the new boarder, and Hal backed the other horse out of Ms. Bishop's trailer. "This is Duke," he said. "He's got a good head on him, but his stride's a little choppy. Still a nice ride. Ms. Bishop mentioned a friend might join you." Duke was a classic chestnut. His neck, mane, and tail, all the color of a copper penny, shone in the late-afternoon sun. Another groom came to lead Duke away, and feed and various arrangements were made.

Hal stacked black-and-gold saddle carriers and tack boxes on the sidewalk, and handed Alexa a card. "Here's my personal cell phone number. Call me if you have any questions or problems." Then he shut the trailer doors, waved, and drove off.

Alexa stood on the curb, watching assistants parade Ms. Bishop's equipment into the stable, and grinned. It was all coming together just as she'd planned—maybe even better. With her afternoons free and the keys to two racehorses, the next two weeks promised to be one big joyride. Now, if only the right man were waiting at the finish line . . .

chapter five

"H er head is *so* big."

"It's totally Easter Island."

"Un melón."

"Let's make it bigger."

Mel, Kiyoko, and Alexa clustered around Alexa's desk, hard at work on the blog. Besides capturing the pizza vampire incident, Alexa had collected less-than-flattering photographs of the night security guard, Emma's butt, and the driver of the Broadway bus. The latter quite obviously had either a well-developed frontal lobe or a very small hat.

"This should be a regular feature." Melanie seemed to have lost her reservations and gotten into the spirit of things. She selected the bus driver's head with the mouse and clicked a few times.

"¡Un globo!"

"A Macy's special!"

"Bigger." Mel clicked again until the head threatened to crush the uniformed body. "There. That should do it."

"Let's see them all together," said Alexa. She selected "thumbnails" and displayed the gallery of photos, earning some hoots and more raucous comments. "Thanks, amigas. I'll take it from here. Don't forget to tell all your friends to visit the blogsite."

"Aren't we going out tonight, lads?"

"Sure," Alexa said. "I just want to finish sorting these. They're all so good, I'm not sure which one to use first."

"I don't know . . ." Mel said.

"Don't worry, earth girl. Even you can get into an all-ages club."

Mel put her hands on her hips. "That's not it! I'm just saying, maybe Alexa shouldn't go public with that stuff."

Alexa grinned naughtily. "Why not?"

"These aren't exactly public people," Mel said.

"They're not exactly hermits, either," Kiyoko argued, glancing over at the open bedroom door.

Olivia knocked softly and entered. "Who's not a hermit?" She walked over to Alexa's desk and peered at the computer screen. "Say, isn't that the security guard?"

"See?" Kiyoko said to Mel. "Public domain."

"Hey. That could be the name of the site," Alexa said. "Public Domain. That says it all!"

"I love this photo." Olivia giggled. "It's quite classic, Alexa."

Alexa had captured the security guard asleep, with his shaved head on the video console. He woke up

> ## 66 Mel would be proud of yet another successful recycling job. 99

when the camera flashed. The second photo showed his startled face and a pink outline on his cheek that read "A-1 SECURITY" backward. He must have been using his badge as a pillow. "Hard at work? Or hardly working?" read the caption.

Alexa showed Olivia the thumbnails and went back to work.

"Oh, Oliver!" Kiyoko said. "We're heading out to Bungalow 8. Coming with us?"

"Why not? What are you going to wear?"

"Dunno. I'd better start looking."

Olivia and Mel went off to their rooms to find something clubby. Alexa finished working on the blog template and reluctantly changed out of her new riding clothes. She pulled the boots back on, though, and they looked great with a straight black skirt with see-through hemline and the multicolored halter top she'd cut from the BCBG dress. Mel would be proud of yet another successful recycling job. And when she pulled her hair out of the twist, it lay around her face in floaty waves.

At last Kiyoko was dressed, having chosen a silver metallic minidress and black patent sandals . . . silver eye makeup that only Kiyoko could wear without looking like a massive sleaze . . . and ripped black stockings, ditto. Alexa couldn't resist training her camera on her friend. "You'll knock them down," she said with admiration.

Kiyoko stared blankly.

"At the club," she added.

"Oh. Knock them dead, you mean. If you knock them down, they might get back up again. And then you're in trouble."

"Since you already have a boyfriend," Alexa said.

"Since I already have a boyfriend," Kiyoko agreed, sticking her ID and a couple of bills in her bra. "But Matteo isn't here, is he? Do me a favor and don't mention him tonight."

Alexa tried not to think about the fact that she didn't have any boyfriend, absent part or all of the time. "Let's get going," she said. Maybe someone interesting would turn up at the club.

Mel met them in the hall, wearing a daring, flesh-toned strapless number that Jonah had obviously picked out, with matching ballet-type shoes. Mel was still having trouble with heels. They all walked down to Olivia and

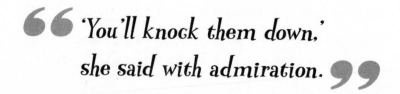

'You'll knock them down,' she said with admiration.

Charlotte's door, and Kiyoko banged on it. "Time's up!"

Olivia stepped out shyly.

Alexa caught her breath. Mel drew back in characteristic awe. Kiyoko just stared coolly.

Olivia shone in a black jersey, but the big news was her hair. She'd let Mel set her pin-straight bob with large curlers and the result was loose, tousled waves. She looked like a model.

"Awesome," Mel said, stepping up to give her friend affirmation.

"Funky hair, lad. Right on," Kiyoko complimented her friend.

They all looked at Alexa for her opinion. She grinned and raised her camera. She was going to have plenty of great pictures of her friends to take home.

ⓖ　　ⓖ　　ⓖ　　ⓖ

"This is it, lads," Kiyoko said. "I told you it was right around the corner."

Alexa wondered how she had ever found it. Nondescript building, no sign—this place was probably too cool to have an address. The storefront windows were blacked out and trembled with the bass beat inside. Two bouncer-looking heavies were standing on the sidewalk, taking money.

Olivia opened her tiny bag. "What would your

cover charge be?" she asked. One of them mumbled something. "Twenty U.S.," Olivia translated over her shoulder.

"Get out! That's nearly double what I paid last week," Kiyoko said.

"Are *you* going to argue with him?"

The guy was beefy and mean-looking, with a bullet-shaped head. He saw them staring and sneered.

"I *am* going to argue," Kiyoko said lightly, reaching into her bra. "Free *Flirt* passes! I got them from Trey."

They tripped past security, more than a little bit smug. Inside, the music pounded, and blue light shone on black-painted walls. Intricate light patterns tumbled across a wall screen and dancing bodies. Alexa could see a DJ on a riser behind a picket fence of heads in one corner. On the other side of the room, a thicker blob of people seemed to indicate a bar area. The four interns made their way toward it through the shifting masses. They came upon a minuscule round table littered with empty cups.

"You lot wait here," Olivia said. "I'm buying. What'll you have?"

"Drink-drinks?" Kiyoko asked. "No thanks, not worth the hassle. Diet Coke."

"Make that two," Alexa said.

"Whatever you're having, Liv," Mel said.

They watched as the bartender took her order

"Can you believe him looking at me like that? From all the way over there?"

and asked for ID. She slid a card toward him. He blinked, returned it, and poured the drinks.

"Can you believe him looking at me like that?" Kiyoko asked. "From all the way over there?"

"He was probably checking to see how old you are," Alexa said.

Kiyoko pursed her lips, as though there could be no other explanation. "Please."

"Thanks. Cheers!" Mel shouted over the music when Olivia returned. She held her Coke up and clinked glasses with her friends.

"Sí. Gracias," Alexa said.

Mel smiled around her straw and made a gurgling noise.

"Charming," Kiyoko said.

There were no seats available anywhere, so they stood around with their drinks, carefully evaluating the scene.

This was no tango club! At home, Alexa would see children, grandpas, and regular getting-it-on couples dancing till dawn. And gangly guys from school. "It says 'all ages,' " she pointed out. "But where are the old people?"

No one answered her.

Where are the normal people? she thought next as decorated bodies gyrated around them. Alexa had seen many of these piercings and hair treatments on the native people she'd encountered in South America. She had witnessed blatantly suggestive moves on the floors of the *milongas* when her family went out to tango. But she surely wished she could get some of these dancers on film: the baby-faced boy in the red fleece vest, shorts, and bright yellow rubber boots; the girl in the duct tape dress with a light-stick taped to her shaved head; the People Dressed in Black who danced either frantically or by expending the least energy possible. As the lights flashed over the room, stripes and leather and metallic stuff definitely stood out. Alexa wished she had brought her camera, like she usually did. And that she'd left the sequins on her top.

"Hey!" said Mel. "Isn't that Jason Harve?" She pointed out a well-built, dark-haired twentysomething, an actor who played aliens that looked like humans in a series of action flicks. He was surrounded by a ring of local girls vying for attention.

66 **The People Dressed in Black danced either frantically or by expending the least energy possible.** 99

"It is! Let's get out there," Kiyoko said.

Alexa joined the group on the dance floor, her natural rhythm combining with what she and Manuela had copied from music-video moves. Lights flashed red, green, and blue on limbs and torsos and whacked-out faces. A sinewy Vietnamese-looking guy moved into Kiyoko's space, and she let him stay. The other three kept dancing together. After a few songs, when the DJ took a break, a tall guy with tangly brown curls walked up to Alexa, the house lights reflecting a flash of recognition in his eyes.

"Hey! Hudson-Bennett building! Right?"

A jolt went through her—someone in New York City recognized her! It was the coffee delivery guy. He looked different in a long-sleeved shirt and not-jeans, with no apron. But it was him. She was glad he recognized her with her hair like this.

"Right! You're in the Café Adèsso every day on my way to work. I'm Alexa Veron."

"Veron—is that Spanish?"

"Argentine. I'm *porteña*. It's what we call each other in Buenos Aires. 'From the port.'"

"Cool. I've seen you with your friends; what are you, VJs or something?"

VJs? Wow. This beat her messed-up-Catholic-schoolgirl image back home. Alexa shook her head. "We're here for the summer. Interns at the fashion magazine, *Flirt*. You know it?"

He nodded. "We deliver there. We deliver everywhere in the building."

"I'll have to start drinking more coffee. My friends and I . . ." She looked around for the others, but they had discreetly faded to the edge of the dance floor. The music started again.

"Do you want to dance?"

Alexa looked in his eyes, and he was looking at hers.

Did she? Oh, yeah.

"Por supuesto." She felt a hand on her elbow.

"OMG. I can't believe you're here!"

Alexa recognized the voice, and again came the surprising sensation of finding a familiar face in Manhattan. Only this time, it wasn't a cute coffee guy with curly hair and dusky eyes. It was Genevieve Bishop.

"What a coincidence! Emma was about to put an APB out on you bad girls; she wants you back at the loft ASAP."

". . . Now? But what about you?"

Gen shrugged and tossed the end of her purple scarf over a shoulder. "I got my curfew extended. But Emma sounded pretty peeved about you guys. If you don't want Aunt Jo to hear about it—and, trust me, you don't—you'd better run."

> **"** *It's just that Aunt Jo has this thing about her interns upholding her image. I wouldn't want you to get in any trouble.* **"**

"Are you threatening me?"

"*Moi?* Not at all. It's just that Aunt Jo has this thing about her interns upholding her image. I wouldn't want you to get in any trouble. Or to miss out on the huge *Flirt* party coming up. By invitation only!" She looked at the Café Adèsso guy all sweet. "Don't worry! I'll keep your friend here company."

He gave Alexa a questioning look as she sighed in frustration. She had to answer to Emma—if she wanted to hang on to her internship. Gen took his hand and led him out onto the dance floor.

ⓖ   ⓖ   ⓖ   ⓖ

It would be impossible to sneak back into the loft now that Emma knew they were already missing.

"What are we supposed to do?" Alexa grumbled to her girlfriends as they slogged back home. "It's not our fault that it's not cool to be seen in a club early."

Even Olivia was miffed. "Things don't really get

started until we're supposed to be safe in bed."

"I know!" Kiyoko agreed. "Why did Trey even give us these passes if they were going to make us late? Hey. That's a good excuse."

Mel quickened her step. "We don't need an excuse, we just need to get back. Emma will see that we had good intentions, and everything will be all right."

"Dream on, lad."

They walked into the loft, and Emma was nowhere to be seen. They milled around for a minute, waiting for the guillotine to fall, and then Kiyoko said, "Well, that's just great. Now we're not even getting in trouble for it!"

"Yes, thanks so much, Gen Bishop," Olivia said. "Guess I'll call it a night."

"Free passes, down the drain," Mel moaned. "Can she really get us kicked off the invite list for the Fourth of July party?"

Kiyoko eyed her soberly. "It's a hot ticket. We're working on that in Entertainment, and word is that the celeb list is so long, there won't be any room for the rest of us."

> ❝ Things don't really get started until we're supposed to be safe in bed. ❞

Alexa balled her fists. "That does it. First things first." She marched through the kitchen and knocked on Emma's apartment door.

Emma answered, looking surprised, and checked her watch. "Yes, Alexa?"

"Well? Here we are."

The other interns had gathered behind her, just to see what she was going to do.

"Good, only a few minutes late. Let's try to nail it next time, okay?"

"But . . ."

"Huh?"

"Didn't you . . . want to see us?"

Emma broke into a smile. "I always want to see you girls; you know that. I'm just kind of tired right now. I'm going to turn in. Is everything all right?"

Alexa opened her mouth to reply, but Kiyoko stepped in. "Just fine, Emma! See you in the morning!"

"Well, goodnight, then." She closed the door.

The four interns looked at one another.

"Gen Bishop . . ." Kiyoko said ominously.

". . . you die!" finished Alexa.

ⓖ   ⓖ   ⓖ   ⓖ

ALEXA VERON'S Public Domain
"The Camera Never Lies"

ALEXA IS . . .
- **photographer**
- **traveler**
- **animal lover**
- **awesome!**

Home: Buenos Aires, Argentina
Work: Intern, *FLIRT* magazine
Hobby: Horseback riding

MY DAILY BLOG

VAMPS OF NEW YORK
Wednesday/ 12:31 AM

    Hola, amigos! Me and my friends spent the night at Bungalow 8, digging the after-dark scene and watching New Yorkers suck each other's blood—like the pizza vampires below.

    ⊠ **They only come out at night!**

Recent Sightings—Midtown, SoHo, a club that shall remain nameless: fashionista Jonah Jones . . . models Shayla Parks, Alicia Chambón, and Riverr Twiste . . . actor Jason Harve . . . a certain someone at Café Adèsso (what's your name, anyway?).

Today's Highlights: "Harvard"— $50,000 Thoroughbred . . . a sandwich of meatballs . . . a really nice pair of boots.

Link | Comments (O) | Bookmark

chapter six

I n the morning, Alexa found a text message waiting from Lynn Stein:

Olivia cleared to work w/u. Come by the mag & get your press badges b-4 you saddle up. pardner!

That rush was dampened, though, when Alexa didn't see her good-luck guy at Café Adèsso. Meaning this would be a single-latte day. She thought bitterly of Gen's timely appearance at the club last night. Alexa had stayed awake late working on the blog, but had never heard the privileged intern come in. She hadn't seen Gen this morning, either. Alexa gnawed on the bagel she'd brought with her and headed for Photography.

Lynn didn't notice her intern's dejected mood. The three supermodels had just been signed for the *Survivor* shoot, and the photo editor was on cloud nine.

"This is huge!" Lynn said. "Or, it's going to be hectic. Truth is, now I'll be busier than ever. Luckily, I have every confidence that you can handle the shoot on your own. But I'm here whenever you need me, Alexa."

That made her feel a little bit better. Alexa accepted the teeny voice recorder and press credentials that Lynn pulled out of her desk drawer. She immediately hung the bright yellow, laminated press pass around her neck.

Lynn nodded. "That thing might save your butt one day, kid."

While they were talking, Josephine Bishop breezed in without warning, something about Christmas layouts. The fashion detector light in her eyes was on as she greeted her intern with a stare. Alexa had put her hair up as Jonah had shown her and worn her new clothes, even though she felt conspicuously equestrian on the Broadway bus.

Bishop smiled in her dead manner. "I almost didn't recognize you, Ms. Veron. You'll do Harvard proud."

Alexa was hoping the horse would enhance her image, not the other way around. But she said, "Thank you. And, excuse me: Which is the bus that runs to the riding academy?"

Surprise somehow showed in Bishop's tightly stretched forehead and penciled-in eyebrows. "Bus?"

Lynn looked at Alexa. "Never mind. We'll put you on the car service account, hon. If you're going to get this shoot done in two weeks, you don't have time to be dinking around on buses." She walked over to the

> **He fell into that confusing thirty-forty bracket, but again, he was well preserved for his age: broad, tan face, handsome eyes, bushy brown hair.**

wall calendar and counted off days. To Ms. Bishop, she said, "You'll want Alexa's work in time for the 'Fashion Alfresco' issue. It's the perfect tie-in."

Olivia was summoned from Fashion and sworn in as Alexa's assistant. She called Emma, who sent her riding things over by courier. Polished yet sporty, the two girls turned heads on their way out of the Hudson-Bennnett building. The next thing Alexa knew, she was stepping into a private car, on her way to ride Ms. Bishop's private horse. What kind of a dream was this?

As they pulled away from the curb, Alexa studied the driver's face in the rear-view mirror. He fell into that confusing thirty-forty bracket, but again, he was well preserved for his age: broad, tan face, handsome eyes, bushy brown hair. "*Hola, compadre.* I'm Alexa, and this is Olivia. What's your name?"

He met her gaze in the mirror. "Carlos. *Mucho gusto.*"

"Pleased to meet you," said Olivia. "Would you be a sport and turn up the music?"

Carlos turned up the salsa station he was listening to and passed a bag of Doritos through the open divider.

Alexa smiled at Olivia. "Now *this* is living!"

"Yes, well."

If anything, Olivia was used to nicer vehicles. She looked the part in her skintight white dressage breeches and white, short-sleeved athletic shirt, plus the long, tall black boots that Alexa craved, shined to a mirror finish. Not the clothes for mucking out stalls, which Alexa did at the ranch, or even for sitting on hay bales watching the horses play out in the pasture.

Alexa wondered how much more Olivia had in common with, say, Gen Bishop than herself. "*Oye,* Olivia. You said when we first got here that you wanted your summer to be normal. Remember?"

Olivia did.

"Well, what is the normal summer for you? *¿Cómo pasas el tiempo?*"

"How do I—pass my time?"

Alexa nodded. "What do you usually do?"

"Oh . . . go wherever is most convenient." At Alexa's puzzled look, she explained. "Mother has a bit of an—obsession with being at the right place, at the right time. So when I'm not away at school, we beat a path from London to Paris to New York to the Riviera, with slight detours to whatever spot is *au courant.*"

"But what do you do for fun when school is out?"

She appeared at a loss. "This," she said, tilting her head back against the cushion. "If it hadn't been the internship, it would've been some other high-profile program to, quote, keep me busy. If an activity won't get us into the society pages, Mother won't touch it with a ten-foot pole." She reflected on that for a moment, then brightened. "So, tell me. What's normal for you, Alexa Veron?"

"Well, first of all, normal would be summer when there is supposed to be summer, in the hot months—*enero, febrero, marzo.*"

"When it's positively freezing in the U.K. That's right. Argentina," Olivia said. "Your seasons are switched down there."

"*Your* seasons are reversed up here."

They grinned at each other.

"Quite right—" "*Tienes razon,*" they said at the same time.

Alexa sighed. "The normal summer for me would be many visits with my *hermanita,* Luisa, to our

> **If** an activity won't get us into the society pages, Mother won't touch it with a ten-foot pole. **"**

grandmother's *estancia* in the country. That is a ranch, yes? And one or two trips to whichever cities have the nerd conferences our parents want to attend."

The corners of Olivia's mouth turned up. "Nerd conferences?"

"Where professors spend a weekend congratulating each other on being professors."

"Right. But you get to travel."

"*Sí*, and we always go somewhere special while we are there, to some ruins or festivals or hiking. One time when we were in Brazil, we went to this total rain forest, and we were right there with the animals. Mami got her picture taken holding a little monkey!"

"You see, my mum would never do that. Unless the monkey belonged to the royal family."

"So, what do you do with your horses all the time?"

"Keep them at school. And then sometimes we bring them home, or to shows. Ellison and Goo-Goo."

"Goo-Goo!"

Olivia looked sheepish. "His registered name is Garrett's Goliath, which doesn't suit him at all. Yeah, he's a big, tough hunter, but he's so soft and mushy when he's not working that I call him Goo-Goo."

"That's cute," Alexa said. "Campo is the same. He can run cattle for hours and then, after, play in the waterhole like a colt."

"I'd love to see him sometime."

"My grandmother will invite you!"

"That would be lovely."

They pulled up in front of the riding academy, and Carlos let them out at the curb. Inside, they asked a groom to saddle Harvard and Duke.

"I can't wait to see Ms. Bishop's horses," Olivia said. "American Thoroughbreds are so . . . different."

Alexa was glad to see her friend wasn't intimidated by riding a strange horse. "If they're as smooth as they look, we'll have a lot of fun. Let's warm up in the arena and see how they go."

ⓖ ⓖ ⓖ ⓖ

Duke arrived first down the ramp. Alexa watched Olivia get on and test him out while she waited for Harvard. What would it be like to travel the world Bourne-Cecil style, to always be used to the best? Alexa intended to find out. But not to let that change her—she would be

66 *What would it be like to travel the world Bourne-Cecil style, to always be used to the best? Alexa intended to find out.* **99**

at home on a private jet or in Campo's stall with a rake. She suspected that Olivia would like to be privy to both worlds herself; the girl had been embarrassed when she didn't know how to start a load of laundry at the loft. Maybe Olivia, like Harvard, could find some mutual gain in a relationship with Alexa.

Here came her horse. Time to go to work.

Alexa pressed the button on the voice recorder that hung around her neck next to her camera and press credentials. "Scouting mission, Wednesday morning, ten A.M. At riding academy, ready to mount. Harvard is awesome. The light in here sucks." The indoor arena was no place to take pictures, but it was perfect for checking out her new four-legged friend before hitting the mean streets of New York.

Harvard was a large Thoroughbred, an unusual chocolate color with a slightly darker mane and tail. A slim white blaze gave his face a refined look, and white stockings ran halfway up three of his legs. His cigar-colored tack—a matched saddle, bridle, and martingale in the finest German leather—suited him to a T.

Harvard gave a happy little grumble as Alexa led him over to the mounting block and checked the fit of the bridle. She reached under the saddle flap and tightened the girth another notch. "Okay, Harvey," she said, gathering up the reins. Putting a foot in the stirrup, she swung smoothly into the saddle.

The arena was basically a large, ground-floor room over which sand and dirt had been smoothed. The brick walls had been painted green and white, and several stout green-and-white poles supported the ceiling. They looked solid—and hard. She moved Harvard into a cautious walk, then increased the pace.

Harvard's gaits were smooth as water, and he responded so well to any pressure from Alexa's seat and legs that she stopped worrying about slamming into a post. In fact, after a few successful walk, trot, and canter circles, she used the posts as obstacles and guided Harvard through them as Olivia and Duke were doing.

"How do you like him?" Alexa asked Olivia of her mount. The chestnut Thoroughbred appeared well schooled and carried himself nicely. While not as big-boned as Harvard, he had more nervous energy, which Olivia seemed quite able to handle.

"He's quick through these posts!" Olivia said, pulling the horse up at the gate. "And he's sweet—he has that look in his eye." The gelding turned his face with its diamond-shaped white star toward Alexa on cue and pawed the ground. "How about you? How's Harvard doing?"

"He feels ready for anything. What do you say?"

"Let's go!"

◎   ◎   ◎   ◎

Out on the street, birds chirped in trees that stuck out of the concrete parking strip. Trucks and cars chugged by. The sound of shod hooves rang out as the two horses walked sensibly down 90th Street to the light at Amsterdam Avenue, which was green. Morning sunshine glanced off of Harvard's brown shoulders in prism-colored rays as they moved along, his neck bobbing in time to his alternate footfalls. It was a far cry from galloping Campo across the Argentine prairie. Even stranger than riding a horse in a downtown building was riding along a city street as though it were a common mode of transportation.

Instead of cattle, sirens bawled in the distance. Someone honked right next to them, and Harvard didn't flinch. They made their way toward the park, with both horses curious but unfazed by two men carrying a bathtub down the sidewalk, a tour bus with a bunch of people waving on top, and a driver who leaned out of a moving bread truck and yelled, "Ride 'em, cowgirls!" The only distraction that gave them pause was an open

" Even stranger than riding a horse in a downtown building was riding along a city street as though it were a common mode of transportation. "

hydrant that poured water into the street for no apparent reason. Harvard skittered on by, none too pleased. But, with a quick drop of his head, Duke snatched the reins from Olivia's hands and took a drink from the gusher. She gave him a kick and made him move on.

"I know you're thirsty, but you've got to obey the traffic signal, boy," she said, patting his neck as they made it through the yellow at Columbus Avenue. She turned in the saddle. "Guess what, Alexa? He likes water! I can't say I blame him. It's so hot, I'd like a shower, too."

"Afterward, *chica*. Afterward!"

They rode another block and then pulled their horses up smartly at Central Park West, waiting for the red light to change.

Olivia motioned with her riding crop. "Well, there it is!"

The bridle path entrance lay just across the street. Pedestrians and baby strollers and dogs on leashes moved in and out of Central Park. Beyond them, past the trees and the joggers and the blue of a huge reservoir, Alexa could see the jagged yet orderly city skyline. She'd seen it dozens of times and gotten a thrill, but nothing like this! She felt like an intrepid explorer, discovering the New World.

All the novelty and excitement of the past two weeks evaporated into thin air. Things *were* different

> *She felt like an intrepid explorer,*
> *discovering the New World.*

from the back of a horse. They were waiting for her here—the pictures she was meant to take. She could feel it.

"Stop dreaming, Alexa, and come on!"

Harvard seemed to sense something momentous in the air, too, for he strode out excitedly when she nudged him as the "walk" signal blinked. *And they're off!* she thought, picturing an imaginary starting gate. No doubt about it. This internship began now.

chapter seven

Once inside the park, Alexa edged Harvard onto the grass, out of the way, while she looked around and got her bearings. Olivia and Duke stood beside them.

"We should really get someone to take our picture together, Lexa."

"In a minute." Alexa tugged at her voice recorder. "Ten fifty-two A.M.; sunny, patchy clouds, light very good at the"—she bent in the saddle to read a bronze plaque—"Jac-que-line Ken-needy Onassis Reservoir. Great backdrop from this angle."

The horses waited quietly as park life buzzed around them.

"Harvey is so steady, he'll make a perfect tripod," Alexa commented.

"Yes," Olivia agreed, shifting in the saddle. "Now, what are my official duties again, boss?"

"Not much right now. We're mostly going to scout out some locations today and enjoy the ride. Once we get started, all you'll have to do is keep track of my spare lenses and stuff, help me reload, run crowd control. That sort of thing. Oh, and hold my horse when I have to go to the *porteño* potty."

"You mean . . . the loo?"

"*Sí,* the *porteño* potty. This is what they call the outdoor one here. I heard somebody talking about it."

Olivia grinned slowly. "Ri-ight."

"Well, let's see what the rest of the park has to offer. You've been here before. Which way should we go?"

"There's not much but the reservoir over that direction. Follow me."

Alexa took up the reins, then clutched at them as someone screeched a bicycle to a stop right beside her, spraying dirt from the path. Alexa and Olivia stared at the man in surprise. Harvard and Duke danced, and the girls held them steady.

"Remain on your vehicles," said the young male police officer, dressed in a black uniform shirt and shorts and a bicycle helmet. He was stocky and fit. His badge read "CAGE." From Alexa's angle, his black mirror sunglasses reflected the bump of Harvard's withers. "You ladies are in a lot of trouble," he said. "Let's see some identification." It wasn't a question.

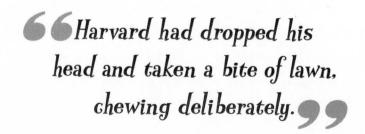

❝Harvard had dropped his head and taken a bite of lawn, chewing deliberately.❞

Alexa drew back in the saddle. Was security always this tight?

She held her press card away from her neck, feeling incredibly VIP, like she was backstage at a Marc Anthony concert. Harvard swished his tail. Olivia showed her ID, too.

The officer's sunglasses focused on the cards. "Press, huh? Well, I don't care who you're workin' for, you get your horses offa the grass."

"Off the grass?" Alexa echoed. Wasn't that where horses belonged?

He raised his voice. "*Off* the grass. *On* the bridle path. Comprendy? You're in violation of Regulation 1-05.q.1: 'No person may ride a horse in any park, except on bridle paths.' " He stabbed a finger at the dirt track.

Alexa looked from the spot where Harvard was standing to the spot that the officer had just pointed to. She spread her hands. "But I am *right next* to the bridle path. *¿Comprende Ud.?*"

Cage's square face went pink and his voice strained: "Do you want me to add 1-05.q.2: recklessness? Now get your hands on that steering wheel!" He indicated Harvard's reins.

Alexa swiped for them a moment too late. Harvard had dropped his head and taken a bite of lawn, chewing deliberately.

" Get out of my sight. Before I add 'unattended animal' when I have you both hauled in! "

The policeman growled. "Off course! Reckless endangerment! And now *damage to park shrubbery*?"

Duke put his head down and joined his friend for lunch. Olivia let out a giggle.

Cage had his radio out, ready to call for backup.

"Please—we just got here," Alexa said, managing to pull Harvard's head up with the reins. "I promise we'll be more careful." She tried hard not to laugh.

"Then move along!" Cage shouted, a purple vein threatening to pop out of his temple. "Get out of my sight. Before I add 'unattended animal' when I have you both hauled in!"

Alexa decided there was no use trying to reason with this gentleman, who accused them of violating every park rule known to man within their first five minutes in the park. "Yes, sir," she said, collecting Harvard and giving his sides a squeeze with her calves.

"We're going," said Olivia, giving Duke a kick.

"Get out of my sight! And don't let me catch you on the grass again!"

So much for the magic power of press credentials. As Harvard obediently walked on, Alexa imagined the eyes of the irate policeman staring armor-piercing bullets into her back. Even though it was an awfully hot day, she wished she had worn the hunt coat.

"That was a close one," Olivia said.

"¡Ay, chica! Guess what? We missed our chance. We should have asked him to take our picture."

They both laughed.

> **Alexa had heard the park called New York's "living room," and now she knew why.**

Riding on, they skirted a wide lawn. Alexa had heard the park called New York's "living room," and now she knew why. Everyone seemed at home here—office people, student types, families, the elderly, folks with dogs, others with kites or strollers or huge backpacks. Many waved as the horses passed.

The park was swelling with the lunchtime crowd when horses and riders approached a large lake. Duke began champing at the bit upon sighting it.

"This is my favorite spot," Olivia told Alexa. "It reminds me of a place we used to summer, back home."

The cool-looking lake was dotted with rowboats and ducks, and flanked by a café and arcade. Even though people strolling by wore the clothes of today, the scene seemed to have leaped from another era. It felt right to be seeing it all at a horse's pace.

"It reminds me of home, too," Alexa said. "We'll have to come back and hang out here with Mel and Kiyoko. They'll totally love it."

"Well, Duke certainly loves it!" Duke, excited by the water, refused to calm down, prancing this way and that, held in check by his adept rider, who kept him moving forward.

They crossed beneath a shadowy bridge with beautiful, curling scrollwork that spanned the bridle path to let pedestrians cross. Alexa felt so tall on the big Thoroughbred that she ducked as they went under the archway, though there was a good meter to spare in the center. "Iron bridge past lake: Shots from this angle might be interesting," Alexa noted on her recorder. She snapped a few camera frames, one-handed. "This isn't cutting it." Alexa halted Harvard and asked her assistant for another memory card.

Olivia circled back and stopped. She took the reins in one hand and reached for the gear bag . . . and it was all over.

> 66 **They crossed beneath a shadowy bridge with beautiful, curling scrollwork that spanned the bridle path to let pedestrians cross.** 99

Duke snatched at the bit again and caught her off guard.

"Duke!" she cautioned, trying to keep her balance as he gathered his legs under him. He leaped off the path and went for the water at a dead run, scattering people and dogs in his path.

"Duke!"

Olivia must have found it more prudent to hang on to Duke's neck than to grab at the flapping reins. The two thundered toward the water's edge, shattering the serenity of the rowboaters and waterfowl and causing the paddleboaters to pedal like crazy to clear a space, should the monster invade the lake.

"Are they filming a movie?" Alexa heard someone ask, among shouts of "Watch out!" and "Run!"

Duke showed no signs of stopping. Alexa pushed Harvard into a fast trot and went after them, toward the boat launch. There was no beach or slope, just a concrete edge to the little boat harbor, where water lapped a few inches below. Alexa saw Duke's shod hooves scrabble for a moment, then push off. Olivia, her hands deep in Duke's mane, went into a perfect two-point position as the horse tucked his legs and dove off the side as though it were indeed part of a script. They landed in three feet of duck-poop-riddled water, with an enormous splash.

Alexa had the presence of mind to snap several frames through the wall of beaded water that shot in all directions. *"¡Qué bárbaro!"* she said, followed by, "Hey!" Harvard had begun to dance in place.

He hadn't liked the splash, or the crazed flock of ducks and seagulls that had become instantly airborne. His front feet came off the ground and pawed the air.

"What is this—?"

Harvard's feet hit the turf. Alexa's stomach crashed somewhere in her toes as he whirled and got the hell out of there at a racing gallop. They shot across a paved road and into a grassy meadow, straight toward a crowd of park revelers: A toddler blowing bubbles. An elderly woman using a walker. Tanners and readers and nappers. There was no dodging them; Harvard did not possess the twist-and-turn agility of Campo, or the cowpony's sliding stop. Alexa sawed on the reins, and only then did Harvard slow down enough to let out a series of bucks, each one higher than the last.

Alexa was used to riding out bucks, but tough little Campo had less bulk and less momentum than the highly bred racehorse. After the first two bucks, Alexa lost first one stirrup, then the other. She fell heavily off to one side, hanging on to the pommel for dear life. Her arms burned in their sockets. Her legs flapped uselessly and jerked her farther out of the saddle.

"Alexa knew it was bail or be tossed."

Finally, Alexa knew it was bail or be tossed.

Praying that the four shod hooves would miss her, she let go, collapsed to the ground, and tried to roll. Instead, she bounced heavily to a stop, inches from a concrete water fountain where a little boy had been attempting to stretch up from his tiptoes to take a drink.

The world stopped.

All Alexa could see were stars and the child's big, round eyes and runny nose. "La-dy? Are you okay?"

She struggled for breath, but her voice seemed to be trapped somewhere deep inside. Her vision swam for a moment. *I'm okay,* she thought, gingerly flexing her limbs. *I just want to see a familiar face. Or my mami.*

"I'm fine," she said out loud, trying to sit up. "I'll be fine." She climbed shakily to her feet, then gasped as she noticed the grass stains on her leather jodhpurs and a jagged tear in the sleeve of the riding shirt. "My clothes! They are ruined!" What if she had to pay for them? Jonah might not be so understanding this time. Who knew what they cost. Funny, the things you'd think of in a life-threatening situation.

The people who were hovering nearby started to disperse.

"Look out," someone called. "Watch it!"

Another, louder voice shouted, *"Loose horse!"*

Everyone in the area sprang in different directions, except for Alexa. Even if she had wanted to move, it took all her strength to try to stay standing.

> **66** *He saw Alexa and went from thirty to zero in three seconds.* **99**

Harvard came straight at her at a mad run, ears back, eyes rolling, legs pumping. The huge brown Thoroughbred had made a broad circle, scattering the sunbathers on the lawn, and ending once more in front of his disheveled rider. When he realized that he'd returned to his new person-of-interest, the panic button switched off. He saw Alexa and went from thirty to zero in three seconds.

Nobody in the area made a sound as the big horse stopped short on all four feet before Alexa, as though it were part of an act. Harvard stood there, head bobbing, sides heaving, saddle askew, and waited.

Some feeling returned to Alexa's numb body. She put a wobbly hand on the water fountain for balance and accidentally activated the stream. Harvard snorted and backed away. Then he gave it a good look, crept back up, and snaked his neck out to sputter his lips in the spray.

The scattered crowd burst into applause.

⊚   ⊚   ⊚   ⊚

Slowly, Alexa led Harvard back over to the boat launch.

Olivia had finally gotten hold of the reins, pulled Duke's head around, and ridden him, dripping, out of the water. She got down from the saddle, a wet-cat expression on her mud-spattered face. Her boots were soaked, and her white breeches and shirt looked like a Jackson Pollock painting. A trail of green slime ran down one leg and formed a puddle on the concrete.

"Well. Looks like Duke here fancies water a bit more than we knew."

"And Harvard doesn't. Maybe he just needs practice. Is there such a thing as water polo for horses?"

"If so, it's not an Olympic sport yet." She surveyed her clothes. "Drat. I think my boots are ruined."

"I think you're right."

"My breeches are a mess, and my shirt is a total loss." This sounded more like an inconvenience than a catastrophe.

"*Verdad.*"

66 *Her boots were soaked, and her white breeches and shirt looked like a Jackson Pollock painting.* 99

"But your pack is still pretty dry! Looks like your equipment will be fine."

"That's all that matters," Alexa said with a straight face. Then she grinned and gave Olivia a quick squeeze. "At least you got your shower."

chapter eight

Carlos looked upset when he saw them get into the car. Alexa and Olivia assured him that they would warm up the horses a little longer next time, and stay away from water.

Alexa had high hopes for the accidental photos. "You mind if I post some of those pics of you, Liv?"

"As long as no one part of my body is identifiable. My parents aren't keen on bad press."

Leaving the park and stable jarred them back into real time. Alexa hoped she would not have to see Gen right away. Olivia excused herself as soon as she got in the door to take a real shower. Alexa wanted to see if there was a package from home.

Sure enough, Gen and Charlotte stood at the loft dining room table, sorting through their mail, when Alexa walked in. Mel was sitting at the table, flipping idly through a Sierra Club newsletter.

"Hey, half off on waxing."

"Fifteen-hour sale at Barneys!"

They all widened their eyes at the shape of Alexa's clothing.

"Fashion alert," Charlotte said.

Gen sucked in a laugh, then asked Alexa, all sincere, "Are you okay?"

"I am fine. Why do you ask?" She checked the table for mail but didn't have any.

Charlotte gave her a *duh!* look. "You look like you got tackled by the entire New York Jets."

Alexa scowled at Gen. "That's what *someone* I know is going to look like if she doesn't leave *someone* we know alone."

Gen smiled sweetly. "Could you be more precise? Say, thanks for loaning me Ben last night. We really hit it off. Turns out we know some of the same people."

"Chicks! Ladies! Suffragettes!" Emma sailed in from the kitchen with a mug of brewing tea and a tub of miniature chocolate chip cookies and sat down. "Help yourselves to cookies, girls. It's wonderful to be alive!"

"You're in a good mood," Gen sniffed.

Neither she nor Charlotte took any cookies. Alexa and Mel each scooped up a handful.

"I am." Emma ate a cookie. "I've got good news for you, and good news for me."

"What's the good news for us?" asked Charlotte.

Emma reached for an envelope on the table. "Passes for all interns to the Fourth of July *Flirt* party on the *Clarissa* on Saturday . . ."

Squeals leaped from every mouth except Gen's.

"Oh. I'm already going. It's on Aunt Jo's yacht."

"And dinner Friday night at a location to be revealed. Compliments of an advertiser."

They all exclaimed over their good luck and/or boring obligations.

Then Mel touched Emma on the elbow. "What's your good news?"

"Oh. That? Well girls, I'm proud to say . . . I passed my driver's test!"

An instant of silence was followed by exclamations.

Gen wrinkled her brow. "You didn't *drive*?"

Alexa said more loudly, "Good for you, Emma. Are you planning on buying a car?"

Emma shook her head. "I'm not even planning on driving, but you never know. It's just something I wanted to be able to say I've done."

Gen shrugged. "I've said that about a lot of things."

"We know," Alexa said pointedly.

Emma gave a worldly-wise sigh. "It's the things you really care about that make the difference."

⊚   ⊚   ⊚   ⊚

They all shared Thai delivery. Kiyoko ordered the

fish dish so hot that Alexa's eyes were streaming, but it was *so good.*

"Anyone want more tofu?" Mel asked.

Gen said magnanimously, "You go ahead." She picked at her larb.

"I surrender." Emma set her chopsticks sideways on her plate. After dinner, Emma faded, and Mel went off to check her e-mail. The rest of the interns hung around, sipping tea or savoring the crumbs from a cheesecake that Emma had bought.

Olivia groaned. "I am so stuffed. I scarcely ever touch 'afters.' "

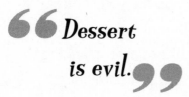

"Dessert is evil," Kiyoko lied, happily finishing her own and reaching over to pick the crumbs off the cake plate.

"Yes, it is," said Gen and Charlotte together. The thing was, they weren't being ironic. Suckers.

Gen set her teacup down. "Listen, Alexa. Now that Emma's gone, you can tell us. What on earth happened to you today?"

"Yeah," said Charlotte. "Weren't you supposed to be out on some big photo shoot?"

"More like a big-game hunt," Kiyoko, who had heard all about the wild ride, said. "On a fifty-thousand-dollar racehorse."

Olivia cast her an *ixnay* glance.

Gen brightened. "That's right! You tried out Aunt Jo's Thoroughbreds! A bit much for you, huh?"

Alexa decided to play her game. "Well, since you've ridden them, you know. They can run, but they can't jump for beans. Listen: Olivia and I make it all the way down the trail, no problem. Then my assistant here says, On the other side of this wall is the Central Park Zoo. I say, Oh, really? and she says, Yeah."

Olivia took over. "I told Alexa we weren't allowed on that side, but she insisted. Said she just wanted to take a peek. That's when Harvard refused to jump the moat."

Charlotte wrinkled her forehead. "Moat?"

"To the lion pen."

Gen scoffed, "There're no lions in the Central Park Zoo!"

Alexa jumped back in. "Not anymore. Not after what happened today. They've shipped them across town. Harvard's got a nice gallop, though! He spooked a little when he saw the lions, so he went for a run. I finally slowed him down, and I would've hung on, if it weren't for the bucking . . ."

"The bucking?" echoed Charlotte.

"They caused quite a stir in Sheep Meadow, I'm told," Olivia said. "I was off with Duke, having a little swim in the lake."

Alexa described Harvard's runaway, her near death-by-water-fountain experience, and the horse's riderless circuit of the people-filled meadow in the park. "Oh, well. Next time we'll be more organized. We had too many things going on at once." She shrugged.

Gen pushed away from the table. "Do you really expect us to believe that?"

"It is the sacred truth," Alexa said solemnly.

Gen was furious that Alexa wouldn't own up to the preposterousness of the story. "I'll just call one of my friends who lives on the Park to corroborate what you've said. If you're lying, Aunt Jo should know that you can't handle her horses."

"Genevieve," said Olivia quietly, "would we be talking to you right now if we couldn't handle her horses?"

Gen shot her a measuring look. "Well . . . I guess not."

"You must ride quite well, yourself. Why not come out with us sometime?"

She laughed. "Why would I want to ride in smelly Manhattan when I can spend the weekend out in Westchester anytime I want?"

Mel walked back in as Gen and Charlotte were leaving. "Hey, Lexa," she said. "Thanks for letting me use your computer. I left it on in case you want to work on the blog."

Now Alexa shook her head at Mel, eyebrows raised, lips locked.

"What? Aren't you still on Kiyoko's account?"

Gen and Charlotte paused, blinking at one another.

"What are you talking about?" Alexa said. "I've got . . . better things to do."

        ⓖ   ⓖ   ⓖ   ⓖ

ALEXA VERON'S Public Domain
"The Camera Never Lies"

MY DAILY BLOG

YOU CALL THIS LIVING?
Wednesday/ 8:05 PM
     I hear the locals call Central Park the "living room" of the city. Would someone please pick up their toys???

☒ **Rope it, ride it, or get out of the way!**

Recent Sightings—SoHo, Central Park, C.P.
Zoo: Madonna's scarf . . . plus one of New
York's finest, who shall remain anonymous . . .
and I could've sworn I saw a lion.

Today's Highlights: getting my press
pass . . . riding a prize racehorse, even if
it wasn't exactly where I wanted to go . . .
spending quality time with a friend :).

Link | Comments (0) | Bookmark

A R C H I V E
VAMPS OF NEW YORK
Wednesday/ 12:31 AM

⊠ They only come out at night!

Link | Comments (27) | Bookmark

Alexa scrolled to the bottom of the page. Twenty-seven comments! She didn't even know twenty-seven people in this country.

"Kiyoko, take a look at this," she said, calling her roommate over.

"Hey! That's a pretty hearty response, lad."

They opened the comments and read them.

> ## Some were obviously from kids who couldn't spell, and some were from guys who had probably tried every dating service and now simply waded through the surf, hoping to get lucky.

Some were obviously from kids who couldn't spell, and some were from guys who had probably tried every dating service and now simply waded through the surf, hoping to get lucky. But one was from somebody who seemed to know Gen and Charlotte:

THIS IS SO RIGHT ON
Wednesday/ 3:45 PM
From: weezie397@earthexpress.net
  It's rare that people are exposed for their true personalities, so watch what you wear when you run into these two fashion vampiras. If they don't like your toppings, they might go for your sauce! (The stuff in your veins, that is.)

  And someone that person knew had replied to their comment:

SISTERS OF DARKNESS
Wednesday/ 6:02 PM
From: kotonkandddy@nycmail.com
         I know what u mean. It happened
to me, and now I walk the night (in search
of my boyfriend) . . . Avoid those 2 like the
plaque!!!

"Like the plaque?" Alexa said, confused.

"They must mean 'plague.' " Kiyoko clicked the back button, grinning.

Alexa eyed her. "This is fantastic. But how could so many people have found the site already?"

"Beats me, Alex. The question is, how could so many people have been screwed over by Gen Bishop and her little sidekick? This is just a random sampling of the population, don't forget."

Alexa returned to that sickening moment the night before, when she knew Gen had won the upper hand. The wench had waltzed off with the coffee guy before Alexa had even had a chance to get his name. "You need to know something about Argentines, Kiyoko-*cita*. We don't forget." She clicked the link to reply to the last comment. "And we don't let other people forget, either."

chapter nine

On a scale of one to four cups, Alexa's morning runneth over with latte. For as she approached Café Adèsso, the cute guy waved her over.

"Hey, Alexa!"

She had planned on stopping in for an espresso to go, anyway, even though the cafeteria coffee was cheaper. This was worth the extra fifty cents.

"*Buenos días,*" she said, entering the steam-filled shop. "Nice to talk to you the other night. Sorry I had to go . . ."

"Yeah, what happened? Was it something I said?"

"Yes. No! It was . . . these rules. Curfew. You know how it is."

"I guess . . . That's too bad. I'm staying at my brother's place in the East Village for the summer. He's never around, so I come and go as I please. I'm mostly working and trying to save some bucks for college."

Alexa smiled. "And that's why you were out dancing."

He smiled back. "A guy's got to have *some* fun." He looked over his shoulder for his boss. "Which reminds me: I wanted to see if you're free this afternoon, after work. I get off early. Maybe we could go hang out in the park or something?"

It was Alexa he'd had his eye on all along!

"I will love to go with you . . ."

He lit up, before covering it with a more casual expression. "That's cool."

"But on one condition." She paused, and he waited. "I need to know your name."

Now a corner of his mouth turned up. "And if I don't tell you . . . ?"

"Ben!" came a shout from across the room. "Let's get that order ready! Now!"

"I'm on it, boss!" He ducked his head at Alexa. "That's Ben Smith," he said. "Have you ever been to the Central Park Zoo?"

She shook her head.

"I used to work there. I could show you around. Sound good?"

"¡Fantástico!"

"Meet me in front of the polar bears at the zoo at about four o'clock, okay?"

That would give Alexa plenty of time for another location-scouting trip through the park, and then she could actually visit the zoo in person. Lynn wouldn't expect her back at the office. "I'll be there."

ⓖ   ⓖ   ⓖ   ⓖ

Alexa alternately floated and skipped her way

to Lynn's office to check in. Wait till her three amigas heard about this. It was all she could do to drag her mind to the subject of work when Lynn asked, "Got a couple hours? I need somebody to scan these prints to disk." She tapped a pile a foot thick.

"You've got it, boss." Alexa could hit the park anytime today, without worrying about Olivia's schedule. Her partner was taking an emergency shopping trip to Manhattan Saddlery to replace her riding clothes. In the Fashion department, this definitely justified time off. "Am I cleared to work in the park after lunch, then?"

"Have at it, kid."

It was safest to ride with a partner, so Alexa would be on foot for the day. She planned to stop by the stable and give Harvard and Duke their carrots, though. And in a few excruciating hours, she'd get to see Ben. It was all set. She took Lynn's stack of head shots down the hall and spent the morning scanning them while picturing Ben's face.

She met up with Kiyoko and Mel for lunch in the cafeteria.

"Liv already split on her shopping trip," Mel explained, sounding jealous.

"What, no Gen? No Charlotte?" she asked her friends as they brought their food to one of the *Flirt* tables. The other one was empty.

"Gen was gone when I got up this morning. I

haven't seen them since last night," Mel mused.

"When you opened your big mouth," Kiyoko said. "Maybe the blog has something to do with it."

"Do you think?" Alexa asked uneasily. She had checked it again this morning: Their entry was up to fifty-eight comments.

Kiyoko barked a laugh. "They're probably holed up in a day spa somewhere, trying to strip every remaining cell of fat from their bodies."

Mel shuddered. "That's unnatural."

"Tell me about it."

They chewed in silence for a while, then Kiyoko and Mel looked at Alexa, who held her empty fork, forgotten, in outer space.

"What're you up to today, Lexa?" Mel asked, noticing that her friend was holding something back.

"Up to?" She looked at her fork, put it down. "I'll tell you what I am up to, *chicas*. I am up to getting my work out of the way so I can go on a date this afternoon."

"A date!" Mel said.

Kiyoko set her water bottle down. "Is it the Café

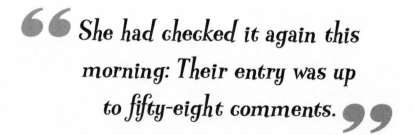

She had checked it again this morning: Their entry was up to fifty-eight comments.

Adèsso guy? The one Gen stole out from under you at the club?"

Alexa let out a huge, voluptuous sigh, nodding. "Only his real name is Ben. He almost got in trouble for talking to me this morning. But he didn't bring up Gen once. Even though he did dance with her . . ."

"He didn't have much of a choice, lad. She basically shanghaied him."

"He could've left the club if he really wanted to . . ." Alexa argued.

"After he paid twenty bucks to get in?"

"Well, I'm still not a hundred percent sure if he likes me or not."

"Lexie." Mel spoke as if to a toddler. "He's been making eyes at you for two weeks. He came up to you in the club and asked if you wanted to dance. He asked you *out,* sweetie. I'm guessing he probably likes you."

Alexa gave a weak smile. "Yeah?"

"Are you kidding?" Kiyoko said. "Gorgeous, talented, from an exotic South American country . . . You're every American guy's dream! I'll bet he's planning the wedding already."

"Thanks."

"I wouldn't worry about Gen being any competition," Mel added. "Take it from me, her roommate: She's mostly harmless."

Alexa's cell phone rang. The caller ID showed

the number as blocked, but when she answered, an all-too-familiar voice came on the line. It both hissed and shrieked at the same time, if that was possible.

"Listen up, skank! Take my picture off that website, *now*!"

No mistaking who that was. Alexa, feeling like herself again, played dumb. "Hello? Is this Madonna? How did you get my number? I didn't know you were in town." She looked at her friends and mouthed, "Gen."

"No, it is not Madonna—you know who this is, Alexa Veron! Don't think I won't tell Aunt Jo what you've done. I'm part of her *family,* for God's sake! She'll have you on a plane back to Bolivia, or wherever you're from, in about ten seconds. You can kiss your internship good-bye!"

Was she bluffing?

Alexa decided she was. If Gen were going to turn her in, she would have already done it. "You know, Gen, your aunt Jo seems to think pretty highly of me. She did loan me two of her prize Thoroughbreds and a private car, so I don't think that whatever it is you have to say is

> ❝ She'll have you on a plane back to Bolivia, or wherever you're from, in about ten seconds. You can kiss your internship good-bye! ❞

going to bother her all that much."

"Don't try to change the subject. We've been getting all these e-mails! Charlotte is devastated. Not to mention furious." A frantic note entered Gen's voice. "Now see here! You took that picture under false pretenses. You didn't ask us to sign a release. I have half a mind to sue you."

"Ha! By then, half of New York will have seen you and your little girlfriend dripping pizza sauce from your fangs. And guess what? I have other photos of you, too." Hearing no reply, Alexa added, "In the morning. With no makeup. I doubt if you really want to share your pores with the world."

The phone seemed to have gone dead.

Alexa shook it. "Are you there?"

"Y-yes," Gen hiccuped on the other end.

"Now, I am thinking you should be doing something for *me*," said Alexa, eyeing her friends. "*Then maybe I'll consider pulling your photo.*"

"What?" she asked quickly, followed by "Wha-at?" as though put-upon.

Yes, what? Alexa wondered. As far as she could tell, Gen's only real talent was living and breathing and spending money in New York . . . *He-ey!* Maybe the wench *could* make herself useful.

> " *Maybe the wench could make herself useful.* "

"Okay, you claim to have the connecs, Gen. You're the one who knows where Madonna and her pals have lunch." Alexa's voice grew forceful. "Tell me where I can find . . . El Torero."

"You mean—"

"That's right. I want to take his picture."

There was a heavy pause. The mere mention of the sexy actor caused women's hearts to stop beating . . . and, luckily, start back up again.

"I should be able to do that."

"All right then. You've got my cell phone number, obviously. Find him, and then call me."

"So, you'll take it off? My photo?"

"After I get a tip from you on where he is."

"No." Gen's voice got hard again. "Do it now. Today."

Alexa could see no reason to give in completely. "Tell you what. I'll X out your face." She winked at Mel and Kiyoko. "Now, call me back when you have something."

◉　　◉　　◉　　◉

Thanks to her friends' encouragement, Alexa's earlier energy returned. She enjoyed a heated discussion with Carlos about prospects for this year's World Cup, all the way uptown to Central Park. It was nice to find somebody who knew anything about *futbol*. Americans went nuts for basketball and baseball players, but all the women in B.A. knew that soccer stars were the sexiest. Not that she mentioned that to Carlos.

He dropped her off near the reservoir and said to call when she wanted a ride back. Alexa said she'd be a while.

The work plan she'd come up with last night was to choose three locations on the bridle path and just keep shooting away, then sift out the best pics for the mag. So far, the arched bridge and the genteel lake scene from yesterday seemed like the best sites, if they could get close enough without the horses going *loco*. Maybe she'd balance those with a couple of gritty urban backdrops. She circled the vast reservoir, noting the light, the weather, and the imposing skyline in the distance. On horseback, she'd be able to follow the best light.

Then a couple of angry voices caught Alexa's attention. Instinctively, she reached for her camera and snapped the lens cap open. A well-dressed couple stood at the fence that protected the reservoir, arguing loudly, swearing and calling each other names, as though no one else were around. The woman tore at her streaked blond hair in frustration. The man threw his hands up in the air. People walked and jogged past them quickly, pretending not to notice.

Alexa set the camera focus and snapped a series

> **"The man, sleeves of his black leather jacket pushed up, hands balled into fists, throwing his tantrum while framed by a big patch of wild daisies."**

of quick ones: the man, sleeves of his black leather jacket pushed up, hands balled into fists, throwing his tantrum while framed by a big patch of wild daisies; the woman, nearly flawless in sleeveless black knit, snagging a dark stocking on the fence, her foot and its pointy black pump momentarily held hostage. Alexa moved off a ways to scroll through the pictures and realized that she'd actually caught the nylon running in several stop-action frames. The daisies and the leather jacket . . . the stocking and the fence. Great contrast. This was definitely location number three.

Nothing else struck her, so she started sauntering in the other direction. Then, little by little, her feet moved faster and faster, until she was practically jogging. "I have a date," she said in time with her footsteps, as though saying it out loud would make it more true.

Her first real date. First American date. Okay, first time out alone with a male who wasn't related to her in some way. It was about time!

Alexa arrived at the zoo entrance, where a tiger statue guarded the area near the admission windows. "I have a date!" she said to the statue. Then she took a deep breath and headed for the polar bear habitat.

chapter ten

I*nteresting place to pick up guys,* Alexa thought as she waited for Ben to show. If he didn't make it, she could introduce herself to the paunchy man imitating the penguins for his kids. Or the acned boy selling polar bear key chains. Or maybe the lump of a person in the raincoat, lying on the grass with a newspaper over his face. How did he get in here? Now, there was a long-term prospect.

Ben appeared, saving her the decision. He wore faded black jeans and a plain white T-shirt, plus Doc Martens. Alexa was in the capris and sleeveless shirt she'd worn for a day in the sun. She had done the thing with the French twist again and then taken it out and left her hair down, in soft brown waves around her face.

Ben liked it. "You look nice," he said. "How was your day, Alexa Veron?"

"Long." She smiled. All she had done was wait for it to pass, so this moment would come. "What about you? How was . . . work?"

"So-so."

"What do you—" Alexa began as Ben said, "I was thinking—" They both stopped.

"Why don't we—" "Would you like to—"

Ben waited, then took charge. "Let's just start walking, what do you say? I'll show you some of my favorite animals on our way out."

Dios mío, Alexa thought. It was a wonder people ever met anyone new. Talking with an almost-stranger made your insides go weird, if you thought about it too much. Especially if you were right out in the open, in public. That's probably why so many first dates happened in dark clubs and movie theaters.

Just be who you are, Alexa's mother would say when Alexa worried about fitting in. But that was at school or a party, not New York City. Not with a guy.

Ben reached for her hand, and now she felt even more visible. *Hey! Look, everybody! We're holding hands!* But she tried to act as though she did this every day.

It didn't last long. Soon Ben was waving his arms, pointing out pigs and penguins and a monkey named Stu. Alexa leaned on the railings to see better or call them over. By the time she and Ben got to the exit at 65th Street, they were both as worked up as little kids who'd been locked in a toy store all night.

Alexa laughed at Ben's impression of the baby

> **"Ben reached for her hand, and now she felt even more visible. *Hey! Look, everybody! We're holding hands!*"**

colobus monkey, pursing his lips with a very serious expression on his face. He broke into a smile. "Total manipulators, aren't they? Like any cute baby."

"Totally," Alexa agreed. "You seem to love them. How come you're not working here this summer?"

"Hours are better at the coffee joint. I'm taking classes three days a week, trying to place into advanced science next year."

"Cool." Now she reached for Ben's hand, and he took hers, pulling her up a paved road. "Where are we going?"

> **"Watch out for loose horses."**

"A little ways. But we could use a ride." He looked over his shoulder. "Maybe someone I know will come along."

"Here?"

"I'm serious. I hung out here all last summer when I worked at the zoo. I know everybody and their dog."

Alexa said wryly, "Watch out for loose horses."

"What do you mean? Hey, wait a minute." He checked behind them again. "Here comes one of those right now. Yo, Davey!"

She heard the clop of hooves.

"Need a fare?" Ben called to the driver of an ornate horse-drawn carriage. The white horse wore a red plume on its bridle.

"Mr. Ben! I'm done for the day. Hop in. Where ya goin'?"

"The lake."

"The lake, it is!"

And Alexa entered the world of *telenovelas* again, starring in one of those romantic retrospectives of what on earth people used to do, back before there were cars. Ben helped her up onto the seat and scrunched in against her. Their legs were touching, and it reminded her of the tango, of home. She got an ache in her stomach.

But Ben made her laugh again, pointing out statues and fountains and trees that he seemed to know as well as he knew the zoo animals. After a bit, Davey pulled the horse up, and the carriage stopped in front of the lake Alexa had become acquainted with the day before. Davey waited for Ben to help her down, then tipped his derby cap and drove off toward his own barn, done for the day.

"What a fun job that must be!" she said as Ben guided her toward the dock. She hoped nobody recognized her from yesterday. "Hey, boats!" Today, couples safely navigated the lake in their languid rowboats or busy paddleboats.

"For the *porteña*. It's the only port I could find."

Alexa's heart thumped.

He rented them a rowboat and they got in, green water lapping against aluminum. Alexa sat facing Ben in the square stern, and he took the oars and moved them away from shore. She watched the muscles tighten rhythmically across his forearms and chest with each stroke, and then he'd push through with his legs against the bottom of the boat. She went for her camera.

"Hey!" He stopped rowing. "No pictures. Please."

Alexa aimed the camera, cocked and ready. "What do you mean, no pictures?"

Ben put a hand in front of his face. "I'd rather not."

She slowly lowered the camera. No one had ever said that to her before—and gotten away with it. But this time, she let it go.

She leaned back with her hands on the rim of the boat as he started rowing again. "This is nice here, the lake, Ben Smith."

"I thought you'd like it. You seem more like the outdoor type than the coffee-and-gallery type." Row, row.

"*Verdad.* This is true. Even in Buenos Aires, I like to be out on the balcony, or in the gardens. My best friend, Manuela, is the same."

"Not me," said Ben. "I mean, not my best friend. Rad is all into scenes and places *du jour*." Row, row. "But he's a good guy. We grew up on the same street in Queens."

"And what about the animals? How come you like them so much? Did you have pets when you were little?"

"I had a lizard. I wanted a dog."

"Me too!" Alexa said, springing out of her seat and climbing onto the middle one, the boat tilting dangerously. "My mother is allergic."

"My mother is a singer." Ben grinned. "That's a joke. I mean, she is one. She's just not allergic."

"Wow, what does she sing?"

"Opera. My dad's in real estate."

"Cool. *Mis padres,* they are boring professors."

"Your parents are? I'll be meeting all of their friends next year. I'll be starting at NYU."

"To be a zoologist?"

"Something with animals. Pre-vet. Then we'll see."

College, Alexa thought. A big question mark she didn't want to discuss. She had no idea what would happen once she got back to Argentina and high school.

> **Though an internship at *Flirt* would certainly be a boost to her transcript . . . if she in fact needed a transcript.**

Though an internship at *Flirt* would certainly be a boost to her transcript . . . if she in fact needed a transcript.

They were silent a moment. The boat bobbed, and a line of white ducks landed in the water nearby.

Ben parked the oars in the boat and stretched his legs out in front of him until his boots were touching Alexa's. "I want to hear more about this gig you got at the magazine. Your camera: Is that part of the internship?"

"How did you know? I am a photographer. I want to get a job at a magazine someday, and go on to work for myself. I'm putting together a series of candids in the park here for my internship project."

"And they'll be in the magazine? I can't wait to see it. I can say I know the photographer. How much more do you have to do?"

"I'll be working straight through next week, but Lynn—that's my editor—said to take the weekend off. The park will be too crowded. It's your Independence Day, or something."

"Yep. Fourth of July. You like fireworks?"

"*Ah, sí,* who doesn't like fireworks?"

"Too bad we can't sit right here and watch 'em."

Alexa didn't say anything about the invitation to Ms. Bishop's yacht. She'd like to see the fireworks with Ben, but not with fifty thousand other people, including Gen Bishop. That girl was just bad luck.

"There's something about being on the water . . ."

> **The moment she'd been waiting for? She glanced at Ben. He had sat back on his seat and was cooling his heels, looking a little miffed.**

"I know what you mean. This is in my blood."

He smiled. *"Porteña."* He took one of her hands and moved in close.

Alexa noticed how a strand of his hair curled around his earlobe. She watched his eyelashes dip as he closed his eyes and leaned into her—

Her cell phone rang. She peeked at the caller ID. It was blocked; it could be anybody.

"I—have to take this," she said, pulling away. "Yes, *hola,*" she spoke into the phone impatiently.

"Hey. I Spy." It was Gen. "This is your informer. I've got that information you wanted."

An electric shock went through Alexa's nervous system. Was this it? The moment she'd been waiting for? She glanced at Ben. He had sat back on his seat and was cooling his heels, looking a little miffed. Okay, the *other* moment.

"Yes?"

"Are you in the park? Get over to the Metropolitan Museum. Fast. El Torero himself is just finishing up an espresso at the café."

"Are you sure?"

"Just get over there!"

"Okay."

"And take my picture off your—"

"Yeah, yeah. Later!" She clicked off and looked at Ben. "I hate to ask you this, but . . . would you mind rowing?" She gestured at the resting oars. "I have to get going."

"What's the matter? Press call?"

Alexa couldn't exactly say she was ditching him for El Torero. "Um, yeah. Lynn wants me over at the Met right away."

"I'll come with you!" He lifted the oars and started pulling on them again.

"No, no. You'll only be in the way."

He paused. "Sure. That's okay. We can do this again some other time."

"Yeah, some other time. Could you . . . speed it up a little bit?"

Alexa jumped out of the boat the instant it touched land.

"Hang on a second while I check in," Ben said, shipping the oars. "I'll get you a ride."

"There's no time! Which way is it from here?"

He pointed. "Not too far, but—"

She was already breaking into a run. "Sorry, Ben! See you soon!"

It was too hot to be running, but Alexa had no choice. Sweat started to roll, then splash down her body. The sunscreen she had used on her forehead joined two of the streams that were pooling in her eyes.

"*Ay!* That hurts!" She squinted but kept on running. Now she could see a corner of the museum, the classic stone structure they had all visited with Emma one afternoon. "Café, café," she repeated, not remembering where it was. She had to run clear to the other side, past the huge columns and tiers of steps, and down Fifth Avenue to the opposite corner. By now, she had a stitch in her side—but she saw a bunch of little white tables with people sitting around them. That had to be it.

She sorted through all the likely male, dark-haired superhero/bullfighter types, but none were him. *Maybe he is leaving!* she thought, quickly widening her focus to include those who were walking away. But none of those were him, either. She punched a string of buttons on her phone, and Gen picked up. "Hello?"

Alexa had no time for niceties. "He's not here! Your clue was no good."

"Aw. That's too bad. Better luck next time!"

"Not good enough," Alexa said. "You sent me on a wild duck chase. I was in the middle of something important."

"Oh, that's right. Didn't you have a date with the coffee boy today? How did that go for you?"

"It was fine until—wait a minute." How had Gen found out about her date? "You interrupted us on purpose!"

Gen purred, "You're the one who wanted inside information."

> **"Not the garbage you gave me."**

"That's right, not *basura*. Not the garbage you gave me." Alexa took a breath. "Two can play this game, Gen Bishop."

She clicked off.

Now Alexa had no Torero *and* no Ben. She should have asked Ben to wait. She retraced her steps, hoping to find him again, but she didn't run into him. *What was I thinking? He was about to kiss me!* All reason seemed to fail her at the most crucial decision-making moments. Then again, how many chances might she get to photograph her favorite actor of all time? Who knew, maybe they'd get to talking, and if that happened, maybe—no matter that the odds were slight—*maybe* he would . . . What? Suddenly become dissatisfied with his life? Leave that rotten has-been wife of his and fall madly in love with Alexa? Well, you never knew until you tried.

But that was crazy. Ben was "a bird in the hand" . . . and he was worth a hundred someones who were out of reach. That's what her father always said when she gave up in the middle of something to start something else: *Más vale pájaro en mano que ciento volando.* A bird in the hand . . .

"Thanks, Papi!" she said softly, feeling as though he were here to give her advice. He would probably like Ben. It had been nice of this boy to think up a date that would make her feel at home. As she made her way out of the park toward the bus stop, she decided to be more up-front with Ben. And not to let anything interfere with seeing him again.

chapter eleven

Alexa added the threatened photo to the blog and slept well that night. So well that she awoke refreshed and finally managed to make it to work with her friends that morning. She took the subway with the rest of them—even Olivia, who insisted on being "normal," in her Harry Hall breeches and thousand-dollar boots, ready for another day astride. Alexa was dressed in kind, because Olivia had arrived back at the loft with a pile of riding clothes in two sizes. They truly looked like a couple of rich slackers, stepping out onto the street with the rest of the office-garbed nine-to-fivers.

The girls left the teeming sidewalk and passed through the sliding doors of the Hudson-Bennett building. Alexa could feel her blood pressure rise, in tempo. And not just because they were planning to stop in Café Adèsso for a pastry. "They should bottle the air in here and sell it," she said as they threaded through the pedestrians zipping across the lobby.

Olivia spritzed herself with imaginary perfume. "*Eau du Frenzy.*"

"I know what you mean," Mel said. "All I have to do is walk in here, and I feel like I've forgotten to do fifty things. I keep thinking I'll get used to it."

> **Even at their most exuberant, Thoroughbreds were more relaxing than a magazine office.**

Kiyoko increased her already brisk pace. "By the time you're used to it, Ms. Mellow, it'll either be time to go home or you'll wind up in an institution." She checked her nail polish, which she'd done up in camouflage, using three different colors. "But for me, it's perfect."

"What d'you mean?" asked Olivia.

"I pay no attention to what everyone else is doing. I let them adjust to me."

Alexa laughed. "This is because you are already moving at light speed." She still wasn't comfortable feeling rushed, and she looked forward to her afternoons in the park. Even at their most exuberant, Thoroughbreds were more relaxing than a magazine office. And today, she and Olivia were meeting with Lynn and Demetria in Editorial, where the hands of the clock whizzed around in dizzying circles. Could a person have a heart attack at age sixteen?

She was about to find out. But first . . .

"After you, lad," Kiyoko said, giving her a push toward the door.

"I'm *going*."

They all trooped into Café Adèsso.

There he was. And he saw her.

Ben waved as they got in line.

Alexa couldn't breathe for a moment. *Did the entire world of commerce just shut down, or am I imagining it?* Alexa wondered as the room seemed to pick back up where it had left off. She elbowed Kiyoko. "Get me a bagel, will you?"

Ben was setting thermal carafes that smelled delicious into tray holders, for transport upstairs. He looked happy to see Alexa approach, but he didn't stop working.

"*Hola,* Mr. Ben," she said, not too loud. She didn't want his boss or her friends to hear. She hadn't mentioned the abrupt end to their date. "I'm sorry I had to run yesterday. I want you to know what a great time I had."

"That's good." He threw in some coffee stirrers. "Because I'd like to get together with you this weekend. I'm kind of . . . busy right now."

Alexa suddenly felt awkward, like she shouldn't be bothering him.

"Why don't you give me your number?" Ben asked.

Okay, not awkward then.

"Sure." She found a pen in her backpack and scribbled her cell number on a napkin.

"I'll call you."

Her friends waggled fingers at him and collected Alexa on their way out.

"See you for dinner tonight!" Mel said, heading off to her post. Kiyoko went looking for Trey, and Alexa and Olivia hit the conference room Lynn had reserved. They were shocked to find wall-to-wall *Flirt* honchos waiting for them. Ms. Bishop herself sat in a chair at the back of the room, as though she were auditing a class to see whether she liked it or not.

"Great, you're here," Lynn greeted the two girls. "We can begin."

They slid into the only empty seats on opposite sides of the room.

Demetria Tish, *Flirt*'s Fashion editor, reigned at the head of the table. She was so tall that she looked as if she were standing next to Lynn, though they were sitting side by side. The former supermodel wore a shiny tangerine tank dress and humongous, teardrop-shaped gold earrings. All she had to do was open her mouth, and everyone in the room stopped talking.

"Leather," she said, and paused. You could hear a pin drop. "It comes from the outdoors, and now we

“All she had to do was open her mouth, and everyone in the room stopped talking.”

are returning it to the outdoors, in our September issue. I'm so thrilled to connect boots and bags to the 'fashion alfresco' concept, where they belong."

Less-than-enthusiastic murmurs went through the room.

Demetria made them cease by sucking in a breath of air. "Nods to Lynn and to our summer interns, Olivia and Alexa, for this one."

The girls waved from their seats.

Demetria described the equestrian look for fall and the tone she was going for. "We'll have live horses, courtesy of Ms. Bishop, and the Central Park location will be spectacular. I'll let Lynn tell you about that, and the prep work that her intern has been doing. Lynn?"

Lynn rose. "This year's Photography intern brings a sense of immediacy and brashness to her work. And believe me, it's not always easy being her mentor."

Some chuckles.

> **"This year's Photography intern brings a sense of immediacy and brashness to her work."**

"The project she's put together is kind of a south-meets-north piece—Argentina meets the Big Apple. Here's a girl who's used to galloping around with gauchos doing . . . whatever gauchos do, yet sharing a New Yorker's closeness to life in a port city, gateway to the world. She's getting all her footage from horseback, folks. I'm pretty sure—Gary?" she asked a staff member. "Has that ever been done by us?"

Gary thought not.

"We'll be working closely with the art department to blend her photos with whatever Demetria's people come up with. I think we're all very lucky to have her."

Demetria took over. "Some of you know Olivia Bourne-Cecil, or her mother, from the shows. It was Olivia's suggestion that we combine Alexa's concept with the boots-and-bags feature, and take it a step further."

They all waited for her to elaborate.

"Alexa is taking fashion candids of ordinary New Yorkers. Now we'd like to turn the tables on our interns. Each and every one of these sixteen-year-old women is beautiful in her own right. We mean to get that energy onto our pages, and what better place to shoot them but in Central Park? We'll pair them with a few of our pros, and *voilà*! The freshest alfresco New York has seen in a long time."

"Nothing like new blood," Lynn added, and heads nodded.

Now the buzz around the table cranked up a notch.

Demetria went on to talk about which models

"Our deadline is insane, as usual."

and photographers they would use and other details of the sitting. "Our deadline is insane, as usual. I'll let you know as soon as we've hammered it all out. Any questions?" She looked around the room. "Then I guess that's it."

☙ ☙ ☙ ☙

Olivia took the meeting in stride. "That went well, didn't it?" she said on their way downstairs. "I'll bet you're keen to take some pictures now."

"Oh, yeah, no pressure," Alexa replied.

They had some fun racing around the indoor arena with Harvard and Duke, and then they rode toward the park again.

"I think these boys need to see more water, not less of it," Alexa said, and Olivia agreed.

"We'll insist they behave."

They rode around the reservoir at a nice working trot. *Off* the grass, *on* the bridle path, under control: Now that they were following the rules, there wasn't a policeman in sight! Wouldn't you know. They dropped down to a walk as they approached the Great Lawn, so Alexa could take some pictures. She shot a grandmother-type power walking in a silver jumpsuit. A ribby no-shirt guy strumming a guitar. An obvious model crossing the uneven lawn in the wrong shoes.

Then, much to Alexa's pleasure, the model reached the sidewalk and promptly stepped on a piece of gum that was melting in the sun. As with the torn stocking the other day, consecutive frames captured the whole sordid tale: the shoe sticking to the asphalt . . . the wearer trying to free it but stretching the wad into a sticky, stringy mass . . . the subsequent attempt to scrape said mass off of said shoe onto ground.

Clouds were gathering when the girls finished up and dropped their horses off at the stable. They had phoned ahead, and Carlos was waiting at the curb.

"Maybe it'll rain!" Olivia said as they got in the car.

"I will walk around with my mouth open just in case."

"Yes, don't let the weather change your usual routine." Olivia giggled.

Alexa grinned. "*Ay,* I'm so glad we are going out for a big dinner. Don't tell Harvey, but I am so hungry, I could eat a horse."

Olivia looked at her as though this was nothing new. "Go ahead, then. Order one. Just tell Mel it's tofu!"

ʕ   ʕ   ʕ   ʕ

To: manuelaferguson@sola.net
From: alexa_v@flirt.com
Subject: another urban report

Hola chica,

How are you and the horses? Sorry I've been so busy. That photo shoot I told you about? In Central Park? It's been awesome. The boss of the magazine owns like a million racehorses, and she loaned me and my friend Olivia a couple for the project. We get to ride around taking pictures, looking for El Torero and escaping from the police. It has definitely been exciting.

And . . . I met a guy. Yes! I kid you not. Muy guapo, handsome beyond belief. He's funny, and smart, and he asked me out!!! Muy romantico, too—he took me for a carriage ride, and a boat ride. Everything would've turned out fine if it weren't for this girl I was telling you about, Gen, the Beauty intern who is living proof that beauty is only skin deep. She keeps trying to steal him from me—I swear! (Find your own muchacho!!!) But I happen to know that she'll be busy on the holiday coming up, and I am hoping this guy will ask me to the fireworks. Cross your fingers, mi amiga.

Oh, by the way. His name is Ben. Love to everyone there (and the horses too!),

Lexa

A lexa made it to another meal on time. The girls had dressed to the nines for the evening, except for Gen and Charlotte, who declined calorie intake in favor of a massage and waxing at the all-night day spa. Emma, Nick, and the rest of the interns hopped a couple of cabs to their *Flirt*-comped dinner at the fashionable Gérard. The seating included a casual showing of a new line by upstart designer K. Leonard.

"Won't it be distracting having models strut by during dinner?" Mel commented as the maître d' seated them around a white-clothed table.

Nick rubbed his hands together. "I hope so!" He looked awesome in a dark blue suit and white shirt with no tie.

"Nothing will distract me," Kiyoko said. "Been there, done that."

Olivia tilted her head. "I'm quite the opposite. No matter how many times I sit at the foot of a runway, I get excited. It never gets old."

"I'm more interested in the food," said Emma, looking formal tonight in a black velvet dress that fell off the shoulder. "This place is supposed to be beyond *nouveau*."

"I, too, am interested in the food," Alexa said, "but I am also interested in who's who." She scanned the room, which was populated for the most part by thin, gorgeous women and their variously shaped male dates. She pointed at another table. "Isn't that Lilia Mendez? The singer?"

Mel craned her neck to see. "Wow, you're right. And look who she's with!"

Kiyoko's eyebrows lifted. "Jason Harve! That boy gets around."

Olivia shushed them as a model in black spandex flares and a bra with sleeves slunk past.

White-coated waiters brought goblets, bread baskets, and news of the house specials.

Alexa tore into the bread before looking at the menu, despite a furrowed-brow look from Emma. "I missed lunch," she apologized.

"Look at these plates!" Mel said as a tray of huge platters with tiny entrées arrived at the adjacent table.

Alexa eyed the plates with dismay. "I hope those are just their appetizers. I am starving!"

Olivia shushed her again, and several of the model/actresses at the next table looked their way.

That figures, thought Alexa. *The magazine takes us out to the fanciest restaurant in town, and food isn't even the main attraction.*

While they waited for their first course, she

> ## *Sometimes, if you wished for something too much, it never happened. And sometimes it happened at the worst possible moment.* "

wondered when Ben was going to call. Sometimes, if you wished for something too much, it never happened. And sometimes it happened at the worst possible moment.

Like magic, her cell phone rang just as their dinners arrived.

Alexa's heart skipped a beat. The call was anonymous—how cool of him! But when she answered it, a sweetly earnest Gen Bishop said, "Hey, I Spy. Guess what? I've got a sighting on your target again."

"Why should I believe you?"

"I can't help that you were late last time. Do you want it or not? Hurry up before the mud sets!"

Emma was scowling at her. The waiter started setting out plates of something architectural across the table. It smelled *muy sabroso*.

Decisions.

"Well . . . okay. Where is he?"

"Not so fast. You've got to promise to remove *both* pictures of me from that website. Tonight."

> **Greenwich Village! She'd have to get all the way back downtown, quick.**

"Come on! He might not be there by the time I get there!"

"That's why you should promise now. Or forget it."

Alexa did not want to give her an inch. And she really wanted a bite of those prawns. But, El Torero! This would be the photo of a lifetime.

"You'll never know unless you try . . ."

Even a slim chance was better than none. "All right," Alexa said, "I promise. Now, where is he?"

Gen sighed on her end. "He just sat down for drinks at a little place in Greenwich Village." She gave Alexa the address and said, "Now, don't forget our agreement! Good luck."

Greenwich Village! She'd have to get all the way back downtown, quick. She turned to her friends at the table and said, "*Lo siento,* my friends, but I must leave at once. An old . . . friend of the family has learned I'm in Manhattan and . . . wants to give me something."

"Do you need me to go with you, dear?" Emma looked concerned, whether for Alexa's sake or the prospect of having to leave her tiny dinner, Alexa wasn't sure.

"No!" Alexa grabbed her bag from under her

chair. "I mean, thanks, but I'll just hop a cab. My . . . great-aunt is expecting me."

She ignored their disbelieving faces and fled rudely, shutting her conscience up by telling herself that a good photographer did what had to be done to get the shot.

A valet flagged her a cab. Fortunately, theater traffic hadn't reached full peak yet and they encountered no major detours. Alexa made it to the bar in only fifteen minutes.

Would he be there? What would he be wearing? As long as it wasn't some elaborate new costume, she would definitely recognize him.

She paid the cab fare, fumbling with the U.S. money, and ran into the club. In the entryway, she hurriedly set the camera focus for indoor light and—"*Ay, no!*" she exclaimed. After this afternoon's lengthy session, the thing was almost out of memory. And probably batteries.

No one asked her for an ID in the busy tapas/sushi bar, where everybody was either rushing across

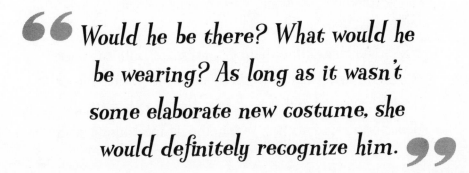

Would he be there? What would he be wearing? As long as it wasn't some elaborate new costume, she would definitely recognize him.

> **66** *Alexa checked each table again. Then waited a few minutes back beside the door, in case he came out of the restroom.* **99**

the bare wood floor or leaning dramatically in to hear what their seatmate had to say. It was easy to see all the patrons in the big room with its open seating. Alexa scanned the place, and a medium-tall man with intense black hair and lashes, and a romantic yet offhand air about him, was not present. Alexa checked each table again. Then waited a few minutes back beside the door, in case he came out of the restroom.

And a few minutes more, just in case.

When the host asked her for the second time if he could help locate her party, Alexa gave up.

I should have given him Gen Bishop's number. He could start by locating her, so I can kill her fifty-seven different ways—

Wait.

On the curb. Waiting for his car.

Was that him?

The suave, dark-haired man stood with his back to Alexa, gazing out into street-space. He wore one of those perfectly fitted yet utterly casual dark suits that Alexa associated with Armani, the drape hinting at a great body within. She saw a gold ring flash on his left hand.

What do I do? Do I ask if I can take his picture? Or do I just take it?

He might say no, she rationalized, raising her camera. She snapped one delicious shot of his strong, appealing back, and then got his attention.

"Um, *scusi*? Sir? Aren't you—"

He turned around, smiling at Alexa.

She backed away. "Uh, no, I guess not."

He was gorgeous, definitely Latino, maybe even Spanish, but about twenty years younger than El Torero. The ring, she noticed, was a pinky ring, not a wedding band. She could see why Gen's informer had thought this was the star she was looking for. Close, but no cigar.

"I'm sorry."

He gave her a funny look, then got in a car that pulled up to the curb and sped off.

> **Close, but no cigar.**

¡Caramba! Again, Gen had won. Pulled Alexa away from an important engagement with some lie . . . But, then, Alexa couldn't prove Gen had done it on purpose. The fellow had been a dead ringer for the man she was looking for.

"Double *caramba*," she muttered, swaying on the sidewalk in her fancy dinner clothes and frustration. Not being able to blame Gen was the worst cut of all.

ⓖ　　ⓖ　　ⓖ　　ⓖ

A promise was a promise, whether she had bagged her target or not. Taking Gen Bishop's photos off the blogsite was painful. With nothing else relevant to put in their place, Alexa dropped in a few of her "art shots"—the leather-jacket/ripped-hose ones. The gum-shoe series with the model had come out awesome, her delicate jersey outfit highlighting the mess.

Double-click! Alexa transferred it to the blog. She kept working as she waited for her friends to come back to the loft and tell her what they'd had for dessert.

ALEXA VERON'S Public Domain
"The Camera Never Lies"

MY DAILY BLOG

EAT! EAT! YOU LOOK THIN
Friday/ 7:53 PM
　　　Overheard between two male diners at Gérard:
　　　Q. How do you separate the models from the ordinary women in Manhattan?
　　　A. With a credit card.

☒ How many calories in gum, anyway?

Recent Sightings—at the K. Leonard showing, at Gérard: Lilia Mendez . . . Jason Harve . . . Lilia Mendez in Jason Harve's lap.

Today's Highlights: chocolate chip bagel . . . taking pictures for FLIRT . . . horseback riding in Central Park—I can never get enough of it!

Link | Comments (0) | Bookmark

Alexa forced herself not to reply to any of the eighty-five comments that had piled up regarding Gen's "morning face" picture: Had those really been lumps of old mascara under her eyes? Could she please report on the quality of Gen Bishop's breath at the time the photo was taken? Would she post similar photos by others who sent them in? Word had really gotten around with Gen's "friends" from private school, her boarding stable, and yacht club. Alexa sighed. All that good revenge, wasted. If only

> **If only she could get a lead on her leading man without Gen's 'help.'**

she could get a lead on her leading man *without* Gen's "help."

She jumped when her cell phone rang. She noted the blocked ID, took a deep breath, and answered it. "Hel-lo?"

"WZOO, you're our fifth caller!" a voice replied. "You've just won!"

"But—you called me."

". . . Alexa?"

"Yes?"

"Hi, it's me, Ben. It was a joke."

"Oh. Okay." She laughed, a little embarrassed, a little amused. "What did I win?" She heard the phone clunk down and the sound of hands pounding a table for a drum roll.

He picked up again. "Tickets for two to the free fireworks on the East River on tomorrow. The symphony plays, if we can get it on the radio, and it'll knock your socks off."

"I usually wear sandals."

"Sandals, too." He paused. "Seriously, some friends of mine are borrowing a boat. We're just going to party on the slip and watch the fireworks, and I'd like you to come along. Southport Yacht Club. We could meet in front, say around eight. Good times. What do you say?"

She would *love* it, sure . . . but it was the night of

the big *Flirt* party, where there'd be lots of star power. Like, maybe even *her* star power. El Torero. She couldn't exactly go chasing after another guy with her date hanging around.

"I'm not yet certain I'm available," she said, which was true.

"When will you know?"

"I'm . . . not sure. Why don't you give me your number?"

"Great. If I don't pick up, leave a message."

"Ben, I—"

"See you tomorrow!" He clicked off.

"Yeah, see you."

Alexa stared at her reflection in the darkened window. Nueva York was proving to be more complicated than she'd expected. What should she do? She couldn't invite Ben to the *Flirt* party and then spend the night chasing after another man. And this thing with his friends on the boat sounded like fun—not to mention a chance to spend the whole evening with him, with Gen Bishop safely on her aunt's yacht in the harbor.

> **Nueva York was proving to be more complicated than she'd expected.**

"*Más vale pájaro en mano que ciento volando,*" she said decisively, turning back to her computer. She'd call Ben back as soon as she was finished and tell him she'd go to the fireworks with him.

She continued scrolling through the day's images, separating them into art shots and potential *Flirt* material. She thought Lynn and Ms. Bishop would like the styles she'd found on ordinary people in the park— the silver-suited granny, some high-school kids in the lowest or baggiest pants possible, a man dressed like a pirate, eating a hot dog. She would run what she had by her boss and her boss's boss after the weekend.

Then there were the few she'd taken of Olivia and Duke the other day. One close-up showed a gleaming black boot in the act of being drenched by the spray, which fortunately didn't reveal the true nature of the water quality. In one corner was the winged portion of a white duck that had been trying to get the hell out of their way. And the boot logo was prominently displayed. Definitely an art shot.

Double-click! As long as no one recognized her ankle, Olivia wouldn't mind.

At the end of the queue, she came upon the photo

"GREAT BODY, it said, *forming the backdrop for the man's casual study in Armani. Great body. Wasn't that the truth."*

of El Torero's look-alike. What a stroke of luck! Across the street, somewhat blurred but still readable, was the sign for a gym—GREAT BODY, it said, forming the backdrop for the man's casual study in Armani. Great body. Wasn't that the truth.

Hey! Who was to say this *wasn't* the real El Torero? From behind, who would know?

Double-click! She could be coy with the caption. "Guess who?"

She gazed at the picture and indulged in some more what-ifs about the possibilities for a romantic relationship. But as she did so, she began to imagine another face on the devastating body. There he was, every bit as sexy and funny and smart and nice as she remembered. Not a world-famous actor. Not a European playboy. Not El Torero.

Ben Smith.

chapter thirteen

The Americans' Day of Independence started with a bang. Olivia burned out a fuse making toast, with an electric-sounding *pop*, and everyone blamed Alexa for it. Even Gen and Charlotte, who didn't eat bread. They stood around the kitchen eating fat-free yogurt and trying to make the others feel guilty.

"I would never hot-wire the toaster!" Alexa protested. "I don't have time to make toast, let alone sabotage it." But she was up early enough today to grab a late breakfast before heading out with her friends. They wanted to hit one of the local festivals before tonight's entertainment.

Emma had left Nick in charge of the loft and gone off to the Jersey shore for the weekend.

"Is that legal?" Kiyoko wondered.

Mel laughed. "Nick's over eighteen. And he's got a hotline to Ms. Bishop, if anything goes wrong. Can't you just see her storming down here!" She did her best to make her face plastic. "Ladies. Ladies. Stop burning down the house. Well . . . if you think it's best for the magazine." She returned to her natural voice. "I, for one, plan to do exactly as Nick says all weekend."

Kiyoko cast her a long, dry look.

"As friends. So what's everyone wearing tonight?" she asked brightly, changing the subject. "I've never been on a yacht."

Gen glanced at Charlotte and back at Mel. "Didn't Aunt Jo mention the dress code? I'm surprised, your being her intern and all."

Mel looked suspicious. She and Gen had been caught in a vicious fashion circle ever since they'd arrived. "Let me guess," she said wryly. "Yellow slickers?"

"Don't be silly. Just—I wouldn't wear jeans."

"What about you, Alexa? Have you come to your senses and decided to go with us?" Gen said. She'd heard the girls discussing Alexa's plans the day before. "Did your coffee boy ever call?"

"Did your coffee boy ever call?"

"As a matter of fact, he did. We're going to a party at the Southport Yacht Club instead. Is that okay with you?"

"Sure, sure." Gen made her eyes big. "I'm totally certain you're making the right choice, a private party over the biggest *Flirt* bash of the year."

"It does sound nuts," said Charlotte.

"That's how you know it's true love," Mel informed her.

"I'm still not certain it's a good idea," Olivia

said. "Alone on a boat with this guy? And a handful of his good-looking friends? What do you think, Kiyoko? Should we crash the party?"

Alexa gave her a threatening look.

"When in doubt," Kiyoko said calmly, "crash the party."

"Get your own yacht," Alexa retorted.

"And she used to be such a nice girl," Kiyoko said. "Look. I don't know about the rest of you, but I plan to start at one end of the *Clarissa* and dance my way to the other. That's going to require mega-doses of sugar. I say we start eating cotton candy as soon as possible."

"I vote for elephant ears," Mel said.

"Elephant ears?" Alexa stared at her, shocked. "Melanie Henderson! And I thought you were a vegetarian!"

Soon they were immersed in the most sacred of Fourth of July traditions, the neighborhood carnival.

American tastes were inexplicable, Alexa thought, and the food names themselves did little to solve the mystery. Elephant ears—neither elephant nor ears. Corn dogs—ditto. To mark the important national holiday,

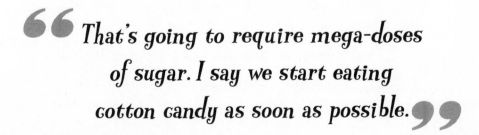

That's going to require mega-doses of sugar. I say we start eating cotton candy as soon as possible.

Manhattanites who wouldn't touch a carb on a weekday consumed disks of sugared, fried dough the size of small children. They drank soda out of gallon-size containers. And they would gnaw at anything served on a stick. Were American holidays only about food?

As they watched a guy on a portable stage work his way through a musical act using only spoons and an empty coffee can, Alexa tried to find out from Mel when the real tributes would start, or if this was it.

"The spoons, they are something from your history, no? Spoons have some special significance?"

"Don't think so," Mel answered.

"Coffee, perhaps?"

"Other than Starbucks, no."

"Music, then?"

"No. Not really."

"Then why is he here? Doing this? On Independence Day?"

Mel looked at her sideways. "Relax. You're reading too much into it, Alexa. Spoons just sound cool. Don't you think?"

Alexa had to admit that they did. Now, *there was a cultural insight. Maybe these Americans are on to something, after all,* she said to herself.

The four interns walked through a midway of games and took out their frustrations by tossing, hitting, and knocking things over.

"Check it out, lads!" Kiyoko came away from the dart game with a black, fuzzy stuffed spider with pink hearts printed all over it. "Just what I needed!"

"It will make a lovely brooch," Olivia said with a grin.

Mel tried and tried, but could not manage to toss a single softball into a milk can. "I swear the holes are too small!"

"I got one in," Alexa said.

"Yeah? What'd you win?"

"I got this key chain with an eyeball on it, but it's broken."

Kiyoko tied the spider to her wrist like a corsage. "Holy tarantulas, Batman!" she said, noticing the time on her watch. "We've got to get going, lads, or we'll barely have time to get dressed. Traffic's going to be thick."

ⓖ　　　ⓖ　　　ⓖ　　　ⓖ

Back at the loft, Nick laid down the law. He wasn't happy about having to hang around the loft all weekend, sans girlfriend. "Go on to the party, ladies. You're free to screw up as much as you like, as long as you're back right after the fireworks. I'll be calling the roll, and attendance will go on your permanent records."

"Jeez, don't let us have *too* much fun," Kiyoko grumbled.

"Hey. Anyone who wants to is welcome to stay home and watch old war movies on cable with me." He had filled the U-shaped couch with various pillows and cushions and was lying there already, watching TV and eating from a bag of Cheetos.

Mel looked as though she were considering the offer.

Olivia grabbed her firmly by the hand. "We're going. Let's get dressed."

Emma had thoughtfully reserved them an oversize taxi to and from the pier before abandoning them for the weekend.

"Ride with us, Alex," Kiyoko urged. "You're on our way."

The van was posted "ABSOLUTELY NO SMOKING" and smelled like a trillion cigarettes. They drove down to Lower Manhattan, gulping fresh air from the small slot at the bottom of the tilt-out windows.

"Are you sure you don't want one of us to go with you?" Olivia tried once more as they let Alexa out at the yacht club.

> ## " She was definitely more at home with rowboats than yachts. "

"Yeah," said Mel. "Say the word."

"You'd miss the party?" Alexa was touched. "You guys are the best. But this is something I have to do myself," she replied, squaring her shoulders and leaving them behind.

ⓖ   ⓖ   ⓖ   ⓖ

Alexa stood between two white stucco pillars decorated with life preservers, trying not to be nervous. She was definitely more at home with rowboats than yachts. *Just be who you are,* her mother would say. She had dressed in red, white, and blue, in honor of the Americans' ambiguous holiday. She'd borrowed Olivia's tightest and whitest T-shirt to top off her favorite old jeans, and some of Kiyoko's toe rings to snazz up her plain blue slaps. Melanie had given her a pair of green Statue of Liberty earrings she'd picked up while sightseeing. Alexa was glad to have these reminders of her friends as she waited alone for her date.

But then, she wasn't alone.

"Alexa. I'm so glad you could come."

> **"Alexa was glad he wasn't. She wanted him all to herself."**

Ben stood before her, dressed in his black jeans and a boxy-looking cotton shirt in sunset colors. How could a shirt look so great on a guy? If his expression were a little more uptight, he'd be catalog material. Alexa was glad he wasn't. She wanted him all to herself.

She smiled at him. *"¿Cómo estás, compadre?"*

"I'm fine, now that I'm with you. I've been waiting all day for this. Let's head for the boat, okay? I want you to meet my friends."

Ben took her hand and led her down intricate plankways lined with coiled rope and coolers and stuff sacks, and teeming with boating types, all out for a good time. He had a little trouble locating the slip—"These toys all look alike!" he joked—and the vessels did look similar with their white hulls and sleek cabins, the main differences being size and number of antenna-things sticking off of them, as far as Alexa could tell. Even a *porteña* could feel overwhelmed here.

At last he recognized the space he was looking for, and in it a good-size craft with a white hull and red trim, named *Lara's Powder Puff*.

> **Even his friends' moms were more exotic than her own.**

Alexa chuckled.

He followed her gaze. "It's Krissa's mom's boat." He helped her across the ramp to the deck.

"Where's Krissa's mom?"

"Bangkok. She's shooting a music video there."

Wow, Alexa thought. Even his friends' moms were more exotic than her own.

"Bangkok. That's probably where I'll be in a couple years," she said casually. "This internship will lead to a high-salary job at some big magazine, and they'll send me all over the world. Even though I really want to start at the ground and work my way up."

Ben chuckled. "Take the money. You can get experience anytime." He waved to a couple of his friends who were coming out of the cabin. "Hey, guys! This is Alexa, the girl at the magazine I was telling you about. This is Jims and Patrick." They said hello, and he handed them the six-pack he'd brought.

"And I'm Krissa," said a girl with carefully messed up hair, dressed all in white, except for a familiar-looking purple scarf around her neck. Maybe Gen's wasn't as exclusive as she'd thought. The girl walked toward them across the deck with a bottle of champagne. "Nice of you to come. Please, sit down. Make yourself at sea."

She giggled. "Hey, will one of you guys open this?" Jims brought some plastic cups over and did the honors. His product-enhanced hair matched Krissa's, so Alexa assumed they were dating.

"Nice of your ma to loan you the tugboat for the evening," Patrick said, kicking back on a cushioned seat and cracking open a beer. He was a good-looking guy with a shock of reddish hair and a gregarious manner. "Hey, Smitty," he said to Ben. "Tickets to the Mets next weekend. Coming?"

"Sure." Ben looked at Alexa. "Want to see some American baseball?"

"Why not?"

He fixed them a couple cups of champagne and then settled into the double lounge chair next to her. "This is the life!"

The water shimmered around the boat, reflecting the pale oranges and golds of the sunsetting sky.

"When will the fireworks start?" Alexa asked.

"About an hour," Jims said, tossing the champagne cork overboard.

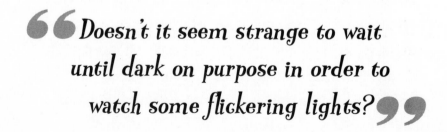

Doesn't it seem strange to wait until dark on purpose in order to watch some flickering lights?

Alexa admired the patterns on the wavelets stirred up by boats leaving the pier. "Doesn't it seem strange to wait until dark on purpose in order to watch some flickering lights?"

"Strange?" Ben said. "Not at all. Just think: That's what people have done in movie houses ever since motion pictures were invented." He slid his arm around her shoulders, as if they sat in a darkened theater.

> **It was thrilling to be this close to him.**

It was thrilling to be this close to him.

"Hey, guys, Alexa here is working on a photo spread for an issue of *Flirt*. She's on an internship for the summer."

Krissa looked impressed. "You must get first crack at the fall collections."

Jims looked mildly bored. "Clothes," he said to Patrick, who shook his head.

"There's more to it than that," Alexa said, wanting them to know where she was coming from. "It's the people in the clothes that are my real subjects."

"People," Patrick deadpanned, mimicking Jims. "No, that's cool! I know a guy who does photo collage, all body parts."

"Is that what you're into, Alexa?" Ben joked.

"Sounds interesting. Actually, I'm taking candids

of people in Central Park, trying to get a new angle. I'm shooting everything from horseback."

"Horseback! Now that's more like it," Patrick said.

Ben showed surprise. "Wow, you didn't tell me that."

"This is really the first chance I got."

Krissa raised an eyebrow. "Looks like you two have a lot to talk about."

Ben put an arm around Alexa. "That was the plan." He raised his cup to her. "Cheers!"

"¡Salud!"

She drank to his health, and to hers—she definitely felt some sort of body chemistry imbalance—and wondered momentarily how Olivia and the others were doing. They'd had nothing to worry about for Alexa's sake.

The pastel sky faded behind the buildings of Manhattan as dusk fell. Boats no longer passed them, but water slapped gently against the hull in a hypnotic rhythm. Patrick stood, staring pensively out to sea. Alexa couldn't help but reach for her camera.

She and Ben talked some more about where he'd grown up and his plans for college until sky and water were almost the same dark shade. "But enough about me," Ben finally said. "You're the one from another country. I want to know more about you."

"Okay, but when are we going out?" Alexa asked, gesturing at the open water.

"Krissa doesn't want to move the boat."

"But the fireworks must be starting soon."

Ben drew her to him. "Oh, they will be."

chapter fourteen

Just when things were getting interesting, Alexa's cell phone rang. It was Kiyoko.

"I should take this," she apologized to Ben, who graciously got up and walked off to give her some privacy.

"Alex! What's going on over there?"

"Not much, now that I'm talking to you. Are you on the cruise ship?"

"Yes. It's big. That's all I can say. There are a million models and actors and socialites crammed on this thing, with more food on one tray than any one of them has seen since before puberty. The seafood is to die for! What about you?"

Alexa hadn't seen any food. "*No sé,* but I sure could use a hamburger right about now. We've been drinking champagne." Which she'd had exactly once before, at her grandmother's seventieth birthday party. Alexa could hear the other interns' voices. "Is Mel there? Put her on."

"Lexa! How's the boat? Where are you guys right now?"

"We're still docked. It's a traffic jam out there in the harbor anyway. I'm enjoying myself right here. The boat is bigger than anything I've ever sailed on in B.A. What about you, *chica*? Seen anyone famous?

66 *But there are hot-looking guys everywhere* 99

"Kim Barnes . . ."

"The actress? Was she with anybody?"

"Couldn't tell. But there are hot-looking guys *everywhere*. And guess who else? You'll die that you missed him . . . Jason Harve!"

"That *muchacho* gets around."

"Plus the whole cast of *Saturday Nite Improv*. But how's it going with Ben? Is he wearing a skipper's hat?"

"He isn't wearing any hat. Or anything else," she joked.

"That's what we want to hear. Listen, have fun. We'll come pick you up after. Meet us out front, okay?"

Alexa clicked off.

"They're starting!" Krissa squealed. She poured them some more champagne and sank down onto a blanket on the deck with Jims.

A purple explosion filled the sky—big spatters of phosphorescent light flung against the celestial canvas.

"Ahhh," Ben said, pulling Alexa to her feet and over to the deck railing. "The purples are my favorites."

A shower of gold glitter spouted heavenward.

"Ooohhh," Alexa sighed. "I like the golds."

For the next twenty-five minutes, they were a

couple of little kids again, the grown-up date pushed far from their minds. Someone a couple of boats over was playing the symphony simulcast over the radio loud enough to be dramatic. The music matched the light show. Rockets and spirals and starbursts collided. Greens met golds and pinks and purples. Bangs and whizzes and screamers accompanied them. As the pace ramped up for the finale, Ben took Alexa's hand and turned her toward him. Then he leaned into her and kissed her on the lips. She returned the favor until the last blast died away. She didn't even mind that her eyes were closed for it.

"That was nice," he said after a moment.

"Very nice," she agreed.

They watched some of the boats on the river head in. Patrick went and got the rest of the beer. "Anybody want one?"

Alexa felt a pang of disappointment. She didn't want to leave, but she also didn't want a repeat of the Gen/curfew thing—not that that was likely, but Nick would be waiting. She told Ben she had to catch her ride.

"I'll walk you out."

"No. It's your day off. Stay with your friends."

He promised to call her and get together again before the weekend was over.

"Thanks for everything!" Alexa called as she crossed the little ramp to dry land. She looked over her shoulder and saw Ben watching her go.

The yacht club entrance was a mob scene. Some of it needed to be recorded for posterity, Alexa thought. Then she noticed that her camera wasn't around her neck. She must have left it on the boat.

She fought her way back to the slip, darted up the ramp to the *Powder Puff*, and spied her camera resting on a coil of rope, where someone must have set it aside for her. She slung it back around her neck. "I'll never leave you behind again!" she whispered to the tool of her trade.

She heard voices around back. She should probably tell them she got her camera, so they wouldn't think somebody stole it. She hoped Ben was still there.

He was, but someone else was on the back deck with him. Not Krissa; another girl. And they were arguing. Well, she was arguing. Ben just looked confused. And now Alexa was confused.

Because the female was Gen Bishop.

She stood with her fists clenched, not noticing

> ❝ Someone else was on the back deck with him. Not Krissa; another girl. And they were arguing. Well, she was arguing. Ben just looked confused. And now Alexa was confused. ❞

Alexa, who quickly pressed herself against the outside of the cabin and watched.

"What do you *mean* you don't have it? I came all the way over here to pick it up. I told you on the phone, I stuffed it in your pocket at the club!"

"Well, what'd you do that for?"

"Never mind, just give it back."

"I can't. I didn't know it was yours. I gave it away."

He was giving gifts to other girls? Gen had his phone number? Alexa felt as if she'd been kicked in the stomach.

But Gen wasn't happy, either. "You gave it away! Well, you'd better get it back. Madonna gave me that scarf."

Alexa saw a shadow on the cabin wall, and then Krissa stepped out. She appeared to recognize Gen Bishop. Alexa sensed an immediate magnetic repulsion. She watched as Krissa stepped between Gen and Ben, smiling condescendingly.

Krissa gave Gen a knowing smile. "Well, if it isn't my old pal from art appreciation class, Genevieve Bishop. Tell me, what—or should I say whom—have you been appreciating lately?"

Gen pointed. "Hey! You're wearing my scarf!"

Krissa fingered the filmy material. "This? Jims gave this to me."

Now Jims and Patrick came around the corner of the cabin. Jims stopped short when he saw Gen, and she regarded him with interest. Krissa noticed.

"Hi-yi . . ." Gen crooned to him, thick with insinuation.

Krissa shot a look at the clueless Jims. "Is this *her* scarf?"

Gen pursed her lips. "It is *definitely* my scarf."

Now Krissa stared at Gen. "Have *you two* been—?"

"No, we—" Jims protested as Ben said, "Look, folks, I'm the one who—"

"Uh-huh." Gen nodded at Krissa. "When you weren't looking. You really ought to keep better track of your man."

Krissa turned bright pink. She looked accusingly at Jims. "How could you? Gen and I were like this." She pressed her fingers together to show that they were once, believe it or not, close friends. But, apparently, Gen didn't hold the friendship in very high esteem.

"See you later, Jimsy," Gen said. "Now, I believe this is mine . . ." She reached over to pluck the scarf from Krissa's neck.

"I'll kill you!" Krissa said, lunging for Gen and clawing at her wildly.

"My hair!"

"Your face!" Krissa drew back a fist and smashed Gen in the eye just as Alexa's camera flashed.

Breaking the dead pause that followed, Alexa stepped out into view and waved at them. "I got my camera, thanks!" She turned to Ben, wondering what his part in all this was. "I sure had a good time meeting your friends!" she called, and turned for the boat ramp. "Gotta go!"

Just then, Kiyoko, Olivia, and Melanie came jogging down the pier. "There they are!" Mel cried, pointing at the boat.

"We were worried when you weren't out front," said Olivia as they met up.

Alexa jumped down the ramp. "Come on, lads," she said, making Kiyoko do a double take and grabbing Olivia and Mel by the hands. "Let's get out of here!"

ⓖ   ⓖ   ⓖ   ⓖ

The four interns did without fresh air on their way back to the loft in the "smoking" van. There was too much to talk about.

Alexa recounted what had happened between Gen and Krissa, and when.

"Krissa *punched* Gen?" Mel asked, incredulous that two human beings would treat each other so.

Alexa patted her camera. "I have it all right here." She winced,

" I have it all right here. "

remembering the blow she had witnessed. "Gen is going to have a black eye, I think."

"Now, let's get this straight," Kiyoko said. "You had a great time with Ben all night until Gen showed up. Where have we heard this before?"

"*Sí*, I know!" Alexa wailed. "It is like a curse!"

Olivia nudged her. "But he was sweet to you all night, right?"

"Tell us more about the date," Mel urged. "Did he kiss you?"

"Mel!" Olivia admonished.

"Well? Did he?"

"Yes!" Alexa wailed in even greater despair. "During the fireworks and everything. This is why I can't be sure about him."

"Sounds pretty sure to me," Kiyoko murmured.

"I mean, I can't see why Ben was being nice to me if he was actually . . . involved with other people."

Kiyoko leaned forward in her seat. "You think handling someone's lost scarf is *involved*? Laddie, you've got a lot to learn."

"How do *I* know it was lost? Maybe he and Gen did end up together that night they met at the club. Maybe he found Gen's scarf at his place later on, after she'd left."

"And she left the *Flirt* party to pretend to get it back," Mel surmised. "She must've hotfooted it over after the fireworks."

"Maybe. But what if Ben was the one who gave it to Krissa?" Alexa worried. "He said he gave it away, and she was the one wearing it."

Kiyoko poked a finger at her. "Then why did he invite you?"

The question weakened Alexa's theories. "Because Krissa already had a date?"

Olivia shook her head. "I don't believe this Krissa would wear the scarf Ben hypothetically gave to her while she was on a date with another guy. Unless she has no fashion scruples whatsoever."

"Good point," Mel said.

"And in that case, the only possibility that remains is that Gen planted that scarf on him at the club that night. You know, so she'd have an excuse to see him again," Olivia said.

"And maybe to dis you," Kiyoko said to Alexa.

Olivia nodded. "That's got to be it. Then Ben asked his chum Jims if he wanted a scarf to give to his girlfriend, and poor Jims said yes."

A smile grew on Mel's face. "Meaning Ben is totally innocent."

"Meaning Ben is totally innocent," Alexa repeated. She looked from one friend to another. "I guess only Ben can tell us what's really going on. But I'm not about to call him."

"I'm sure he'll phone," Olivia soothed her.

"Either way, I hold Gen responsible," Alexa said.

ⓖ   ⓖ   ⓖ   ⓖ

Ben hadn't tried to call Alexa and explain, though it *was* late when they got back to the loft. He could've text messaged her . . . if he was innocent. There was no way to know for sure whether Gen had planted the scarf on purpose, or whether Ben had given the scarf to Jims, or what. And Alexa didn't care. She had to funnel her anger and fears somewhere. Gen mixing Ben up in this went over the bounds of common decency. Right now, all Alexa wanted was revenge.

Her friends gave her ready support.

"It's called 'damage control,' " Kiyoko said, gazing at Alexa's computer screen.

"It's called 'insurance,' " Olivia countered.

Mel grinned. "It's called 'she totally deserves it.' "

Double-click! Alexa dropped the Gen vs. Krissa photo into the place of honor on the blog and gave it an elaborate border. She threw a set of empty quotation marks beneath it. "*Pues,* Melanie? Will you do the honors? And Kiyoko, lad? Don't you think it needs some sound effects?"

"Don't call me lad, Alex."

"Don't call me Alex, lad."

"You're in a rare mood, Alexa," Olivia noted. "You must be running on pure adrenaline."

"So was she." Alexa pointed to Krissa and her forceful fist on the screen.

"I'll tell you what. We're lucky we slammed out of there before any police got involved," Kiyoko said. "My visa status is kind of iffy right now."

"We're lucky we got out of there before Gen decided to hit back," Alexa said. "She's small, but I'll bet she's strong."

Olivia pointed to the screen. "Hence the insurance. Now, what shall we call it?"

Melanie closed her eyes and raised her head as though channeling. " 'Southport Fight Club: Have you got what it takes?' "

Alexa grinned and typed. "Seems like Gen has made a lot of friends in this town—and then stomped them into the ground. If I can get ahold of Krissa's address, I'll e-mail her. By Monday, this photo will be out there, copied in a million e-mails!"

> 66 *I'll tell you what. We're lucky we slammed out of there before any police got involved. My visa status is kind of iffy right now.* 99

Mel gave a little warning hum, backpedaling again. "I don't kno-ow. A nice, anonymous post is one thing. Widespread publicity is another."

"That's what you said the first time, and nothing happened!"

"You only started a war."

"I didn't start anything," Alexa said, knowing that wasn't true. So maybe posting the first photo of Gen and Charlotte had been slightly unwarranted, but this latest incident surely deserved payback. Making the photo public would ensure that Gen wouldn't try to hurt Alexa again; her credibility would be ruined. "Insurance is all it is," she said.

"It seems kind of mean," Mel said. "That'd be stooping to her level."

"Good on ya, mate," Kiyoko praised Alexa. "Go for it. 'Mean' is Gen's middle name."

"You're both right," Olivia said. "Yes, she's loathsome and disgusting, but no, Alexa's not. This could change all that." She smiled at her Argentine friend. "But you do what you have to do."

Alexa thought about her first date with Ben—interrupted. She remembered how Gen had made her feel at the club—frustrated and embarrassed. And now she had ruined what had been a beautiful evening.

"*Sí*. I'll do what I have to do," Alexa said shortly. She clicked on the box that initiated the file upload to the site. "We do not forget. Make no mistake about that, Gen Bishop."

ALEXA VERON'S Public Domain
"The Camera Never Lies"

MY DAILY BLOG

ROCKETS RED GLARE
Saturday/ 11:09 PM

The war for independence is not over in Manhattan (see photo). Today I discovered that the past is not as important to some people as the right-now. For instance, one day you may be friends with someone, the next day you may want to kick their butt for stealing your boyfriend. Poof! Your friendship is history.

☒ Southport Fight Club: Have you got what it takes?

I think this is the reason that foods such as fried things, popcorn, and cotton candy are so popular on traditional holidays—you have to eat them right away or they're no good. There's no time for them to rot.

Recent Sightings—rumor has it, aboard the
SS *Clarissa*, at the biggest *Flirt* magazine bash
of the year: Kim Barnes . . . cast of *Saturday
Nite Improv* . . . who else?, that swinging man
about town, Jason Harve.
Today's Highlights: an elephant's ear . . . a
private kiss from ? . . . about fifty of those
glittery gold fireworks.

Link | Comments (0) | Bookmark

"**O**ut of my way, people, I've got a date with destiny!" Jonah Jones strode toward The Closet, knocking aside temporary workers and rickety mail carts.

Five of the six interns stood waiting for him, practically salivating with eagerness to gain Closet entrance. It was time for Jonah to work his magic on the Boots-and-Bags shoot.

He was on his cell phone headset as he met them in the hall. He grabbed Mel by the hand and pulled her, continuing to talk, past the other interns, who followed.

"Tell her to order the Beaujolais." He listened. "No. No. You don't buy alcohol because it has an animal on the label. Unless it's Wild Turkey, you're getting screwed." He signed off and faced the girls. "My birthday party," he explained. "I'll be twenty-nine."

"Funny," murmured Olivia. "That's how old my mother claims to be each year."

Jonah stabbed her with a look. "And someday, sweetie, so will you."

He led them through the aisles, pointing out a Donna Karan here and Hermès there, to the shoes and accessories territory near the back of the warehouse.

Charlotte gasped and started holding shoes up to her feet to see if they were her size.

"I am never leaving," Kiyoko said, diving for a rack of belts.

"We'll have sushi sent in," Jonah promised. "But first I need a look at you. All of you. Drop the merchandise!" He waved them over to the corner. "Up against the wall. Let's see what we've got to work with."

Kiyoko pushed Mel, who pushed her back, and Olivia took Alexa's hand and swung it. Charlotte swayed nervously, unused to being on the fringes.

Jonah stood back. "Settle down! It's like watching kittens claw their way out of a sack."

As if a veil had dropped, his face went deadly serious. "Think leather, think legs . . ." He rubbed his ultrasmooth chin. "Why is it all so humdrum, so lifeless, so *bor*-ing?"

"He must be talking about you, Melvin," Kiyoko said, and got slapped for it.

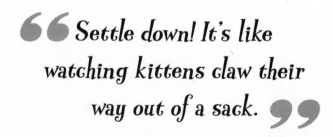

" Settle down! It's like watching kittens claw their way out of a sack. "

"Mesdames."

Jonah's tone of voice got their attention. He walked over to them, nodding decisively. "I have one word to say to you, and that's: C-O-L-O-R." He snapped his fingers rapidly in front of Alexa's face. "You see a brown cow, a black sheep, a spotted pig, what do you see?"

"Dinner," she replied, and Kiyoko high-fived the air.

"I'll tell you what you see," Jonah said, ignoring them. "You see boredom, you see monotony, you see all the tediousness of everyday life worn on the backs of unsuspecting farm animals."

"Kinky," Olivia murmured.

"Not kinky!" Jonah waved his arms. "Absolutely not kinky!" He looked her in the eye and said, "Color is kinky." He spun around and walked off a few paces. "Color is kinky, that's it. That's the concept. Black and brown are dead, dead." He smiled hugely. "Boots and bags in yummy colors for fall. Nothing earth-toned. Pomegranate and kiwi. Mango and pineapple. Lemon and lime."

"Sounds like Häagen-Dazs," Charlotte commented.

"Is that a problem?"

"No arguments here," said Kiyoko, who was wearing a fuchsia and yellow paisley dress over her combat boots.

66 Will you for once just trust people's instincts? Jonah here is a professional. 99

"And the colors will show up divinely against the white noise of the horses' coats," Jonah explained, *"elevating* the lowly black and brown to a heretofore unforeseen level."

Mel stared at him, dubious.

"Trust me," Jonah told her, "it'll work."

"That may be . . ." Mel said slowly.

"No, he's dead-on about the contrast," Olivia put in.

"And that thing about the farm animals," Kiyoko added.

"I'm just saying . . ."

Alexa could tell that Mel was backpedaling again, the way she had flip-flopped on promoting the website. "Mel," she said, "will you for once just trust people's instincts? Jonah here is a professional."

Melanie shook her head. "It doesn't matter to me *what* color the boots and bags are, as long as they're real leather."

Now Jonah flinched, as though stung by having his reputation impugned. "Of course they're *real* leather!"

"I won't be able to go through with the shoot,

then," Mel said, pouting.

The girls were all incredibly excited to have their very own feet, shoulders, and arms featured in this spread. That was, if Mel's hippy-dippy convictions didn't get in the way.

Alexa was mystified. "You Americans have the strangest ideals."

"I'm not being American about it. I'm being vegetarian about it." Mel stared from face to face. "Don't you get it? I'm a vegetarian. I don't wear leather!"

"What?" Alexa had thought not eating beef showed excessive restraint, but not wearing leather? She couldn't even imagine. "*¡Madre de Dios!* Then what do you do for shoes?"

Mel stuck out her canvas tennies.

"Oh."

"I hear where you're coming from," Olivia said quietly.

Jonah wiped at imaginary egg on his face, then turned it around and made it work for him. "I owe you an apology, Melanie dear. M-wahhh!" he said, throwing her a giant kiss. "Perfect angle! Why didn't I think of it? Hit the alternative crowd. PVC and microfiber. Cordura and rubber. 'Boots and bags for the vegan on the run'!"

🌀   🌀   🌀   🌀

" Some people wouldn't wear dead cow on their feet; some people wouldn't think twice about it. "

You learn something new every day, Alexa thought. Some people wouldn't wear dead cow on their feet; some people wouldn't think twice about it. Now that Mel had mentioned it, Alexa could see her point. She didn't share that view . . . but to each her own. Perhaps this was what the folks back home meant about her gaining some maturity from this experience.

But maturity would get her only so far. She went back to the loft and started to finalize her portfolio, to show Lynn and Ms. Bishop the following day. If she could pull this off, she might have a chance at making something of this internship, at finding El Torero, maybe even getting another chance to kiss Ben . . . She popped the photo CD out of her computer and stuck it in an envelope to take with her tomorrow. Then she went down to the laundry room to check on her pants, worrying again that Ben hadn't called. The weekend had passed, and he hadn't been at work in the morning. It didn't seem right to call him and demand an explanation.

The other girls had gone clubbing, but someone was in the little alcove off the kitchen that housed the washer and dryer, talking on the phone. The male voice was muffled by the tumbling of Alexa's clothes. "Dude!" It sounded like Nick. "You've gotta check out this picture of Gen. I'll e-mail you the URL. It's straight out of World Wrestling or something. The Female Rock meets Gen Bishop. I'm downloading it, for blackmail purposes. Might even send it to old J. B. herself." He listened. "Hey, you live around the Bishops long enough, you want to be able to buy or trade some intelligence." He paused, listening, then laughed long and hard. "I'm just saying. If it's in the public domain, it's fair game."

Alexa crept back through the kitchen and upstairs without gathering her laundry.

Fair game! That's what she had thought. Taking candid pictures used to make her feel sharp, proud of her quick reflexes and eye for the truth of a situation. If people didn't like it, well, that was because they were reluctant to look at themselves as others saw them, as who they really were. Normally, she would have been thrilled by Nick's reaction. Raw photo, raw moment, the website a hit, people telling their friends . . . But hearing Nick talk glibly about Gen's vulnerable moment didn't

> **"** *Hey, you live around the Bishops long enough, you want to be able to buy or trade some intelligence.* **"**

make Alexa feel like some avant-garde artist or savvy social critic. It didn't give her a vengeful thrill. It just made her feel mean.

What could she do? She couldn't just take Gen's picture off the blog—it was too late already, and without it, Gen would start the whole cycle over again. With that option closed, there was really only one thing Alexa could do to try to shore up her battered karma. She was going to have to see a man about a horse.

She reached for her cell phone, then sifted through her desk drawer for the scrap of paper she was looking for.

      6   6   6   6

"Sacre merde!" Kiyoko cursed as Alexa turned off her alarm. Kiyoko had been lying on top of her bed, asleep in her clothes.

"What happened to you?" Alexa asked sleepily.

Kiyoko groaned and unzipped her boots. "Late night. We got back from the club and you were already asleep. Olivia had a bottle of brandy smuggled from her cousin twice removed, and we were playing Monopoly in her room for drinks. You missed the fun."

"It sounds like fun," Alexa said, buttoning her jeans and shoving her feet in her sandals. It was too early to worry about work clothes. "But don't forget, we have a photo shoot today."

Kiyoko got back into bed, still in her dress. "Yeah, right. Ten o'clock. I'll be there." She pulled up the covers and rolled over.

Gen Bishop had been hiding in her room, the bathroom, and the back room at the all-night day spa all week, trying to keep her black eye a secret. But Alexa knew she would have to come out of her hole today. The chance to model would surely take precedence over keeping the evidence of her fight with Krissa a secret. Anyhow, the only people who didn't know about it were the ones who hadn't read the blog. And, judging by the flurry of comments, there weren't many of those.

For once, Alexa made it to the office ahead of time. Her jeans wouldn't be an issue yet; she was going only as far as Café Adèsso. She had to know about Ben, one way or the other. She took the escalators through the nearly empty building.

It was so early that the shop was still dark. Alexa didn't know what time Ben got in, but she'd be there waiting for him. *I could use a cup of coffee,* she thought ruefully. Oh, well.

Ben walked up to the café with that impersonal face people wear when they don't know that anybody is watching them. Alexa said softly, "Hi, Ben," and watched the lights come on in his eyes, then dim.

"Uh, hey, Alexa." He fumbled some keys out of

his pocket.

"We were supposed to do something else this weekend," she said. "You didn't call."

He colored slightly, then turned the key in the lock and pushed the door open. "I wasn't sure you wanted me to." He hesitated. "Come in?"

Alexa nodded and followed him.

He flipped on a bunch of lights, moved behind the counter, and started measuring coffee for the urns. "I didn't want to make things worse, what with the fight and all. I didn't know how tight you were with this Gen Bishop. She didn't say much about you the one time I met her."

"Figures." Alexa leaned her elbows on the counter and watched Ben work, dumping fresh water in the pots and filling the cream and milk carafes.

"She must've stuck that scarf in my pocket for an excuse—you know, so I'd have to see her again to give it back."

"So why didn't you?"

"Was I going to ask *you* for her number? No way! It was you I wanted to see in the first place."

This sank in deeply and made Alexa feel warm.

"I wasn't planning on getting in touch with Gen. So . . . anyway . . . I guess what it comes down to is, I sort of gave your friend's scarf to my friend. Who ended up giving it to his girlfriend. I didn't want the thing."

" She wanted to do that.
More than anything. "

Alexa chuckled. "Madonna didn't even want that scarf." Then she gave a frown. "Only, how was it that Gen called to ask you about it? I mean, you didn't give her your number, right?"

Now Ben frowned. "Hey. I said I wasn't planning to see her again. She called me here at work, Alexa."

"Sure," Alexa said a little too quickly. "Right."

He eyed her. "Look, if you don't believe me . . . I really would like to see you again."

Alexa wanted to believe him. But what if deep down his real feelings were for Gen? What if he had been acting all along?

Two of the other barristas entered the shop and called good morning.

Ben sighed. "I'll tell you what, Alexa. I've got to get to work now. If you want to give it another shot, maybe work things out, meet me in front of the polar bears again today after work. Four o'clock."

She wanted to do that. More than anything. She just couldn't be sure where he was coming from. "I'll have to see," she said and headed for the door.

chapter sixteen

"**H**mmm . . . Next."

"How about this one? This has good diagonals." Lynn drew an imaginary line in the air above her computer monitor. "What do you think?"

"Hmmm . . . It just doesn't do anything for me." Ms. Bishop wheeled the chair back from Lynn's desk, folded her arms, and riffled her fingers against them as though impatient for something—perhaps for Alexa to get on a plane and leave that fair city forever.

"Maybe Alexa can enlighten us," Lynn said, somewhat desperately. "What's behind these pictures? Is there something we're missing?" She wanted her intern to succeed, but her butt was on the line, too.

"Behind the pictures?" This seemed obvious to Alexa. "Is the scenery."

"No, the *idea* behind them."

"The theme, if you will," Bishop interjected. "In other words, Ms. Veron, if there is a theme, what is it?"

Alexa cleared her throat. "Just how crazy the different

styles of New York look, especially to a horse."

They let this sink in.

"So, it's that simple," Lynn stated.

"That simplistic," Bishop corrected her. "Everything looks crazy to a horse! Especially to a Thoroughbred."

"But this is exactly my point," Alexa said. "Even though it was difficult for the horse to approach these things, without him I wouldn't have been able to get the angles. Or the access—people are . . . less *guardado* with someone on a horse. You should know that." Alexa blinked at her benefactor, who owned a whole string of them. "If you don't like these photos, though, I have more . . ."

Ms. Bishop waved her hand at an invisible fly. "If I don't like these, why would I want to see more?" She cocked her head at Lynn. "Perhaps we should cut our losses and scrap the project now."

Alexa felt a stab of fear. "Then . . . what will I do?" she dared to ask.

"Do?" Bishop echoed. She gave an empty laugh. "Why, you wouldn't even have to stay."

Alexa felt her face start to crumble. Lynn reached over and touched a hand to her shoulder, then glanced at Ms. Bishop.

The CEO waved a hand. "Well, she could finish out the internship in the circulation department, or something."

"Technically, Alexa has until the end of the week to turn in something acceptable." Lynn smiled supportively. "Let's put the decision off a day or two. Why don't you e-mail us something else, Alexa, hon, and we'll talk again later."

They dismissed her.

She left the room on weak legs. On what should have been the brightest morning of her internship so far, the worst possible clouds of doom gathered directly overhead, threatening to spill. What if the magazine sent her home? Could she even change her plane tickets by a whole month? Or would she have to live on the streets until it was time to fly home? Kiyoko would bring her bread, and Olivia might bring her something to drink, but what would she do for air conditioning? The weather had gotten hotter, and the gathering clouds suggested rain. The humidity level brought to mind that Brazilian rain forest she'd visited. Maybe that was how she'd be reduced to earning her living—taking pictures of tourists holding monkeys.

She should have known this would happen.

Something wasn't clicking when she took those easygoing park portraits—they were too soft. No edge.

Something wasn't clicking when she took those easygoing park portraits—they were too soft. No edge. Alexa knew that Josephine Bishop hadn't created an empire by running weak photography in the magazine. By not pushing the limits. It seemed that even the creative world had rules.

There wasn't time to fix what was broken now. Jonah and Demetria's crew expected the girls in wardrobe promptly at ten, along with the rest of the Boots-and-Bags models. Lynn, Ms. Bishop, and her photography career would have to wait.

ⓖ   ⓖ   ⓖ   ⓖ

"Hello again, Ms. Veron. Thanks for your phone call." Hal led Harvard out of a black six-horse trailer with gold trim and the Bishop signature. Duke already stood tied outside the rig. "I've brought the mare along, like you asked."

Alexa reached up and gave Harvard's neck a scratch.

Hal tied him to the trailer. "How'd Harvard do for you, then?"

Alexa grinned. "He has made life exciting!" She introduced Hal to Kiyoko, Mel, Olivia, and Charlotte. "And you know Gen . . ."

Hal nodded, stepped back into the trailer, and

emerged with a pretty, dapple gray mare. "Miss . . . ?"

Gen, who was wearing large, plastic-frame sunglasses, let out a breath. "Buttons!" she shrieked in a voice she probably hadn't used since she was a little girl. She ran over and hugged the horse around the neck. "I'm so happy to see you!" she cooed.

Alexa looked at Olivia, who nodded ever so slightly. The girl did have a heart after all. Rusty from lack of use, but still there.

A ways off, Jonah's frantic voice sailed out of the dresser's tent. Apparently, the professional models were being difficult. Jonah had already given Alexa and the other interns strict orders not to get grass stains on their light-colored boots, not to rumple their clothes, and not to move.

"Don't move?" echoed Kiyoko. "*No problema.* I'm having the worst hangover of my life."

"I'm having the only hangover of my life," countered Mel. "Ugh . . . my stomach . . . Remember I kept saying that brandy tastes just like a mixture of Diet Coke and Mountain Dew?"

Olivia looked none the worse for wear. "What's the matter with you two? You'd think you'd never got boiled before."

Kiyoko scowled, then winced. "My forehead just fell off."

"I have to pee again," Mel said.

"It's your own fault!" Alexa said. "You didn't have to stay up all night drinking. I was in bed by ten."

"So you could get up before dawn and ambush your coffee man. Any luck on that front, lad?"

Alexa grinned.

Kiyoko understood. "*Muy de la banana,* girlfriend!"

Mel nodded over at Gen, still petting her mare. "What's that all about?" she asked Alexa.

Alexa ducked her chin. "Ah, I was feeling a little bit guilty."

"Why?" Kiyoko peered at her through Visine-drenched eyes. "You didn't give her a black eye."

"Well, I didn't have to publish it online, either. It was too late to erase that damage, so I thought maybe if I could do something nice . . ."

Kiyoko folded her arms. "I think posting that shot shows you have *cojones*. It was a tough editorial call, but it was yours to make. You happened to be there with your camera at a spontaneous moment. You were only doing your job. That's what you're all *about,* lad." She elbowed Mel. "Granola girl here is just jealous that you got back at Gen Bishop."

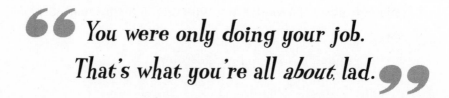

You were only doing your job. That's what you're all *about,* lad.

Mel gave a wry grin. "Maybe, a little bit. What goes around comes around."

Alexa chuckled. "You can say that again. Today someone else will be taking pictures of me."

Jonah strode toward them. "Ready to turn the boots-and-bags world on its collective ear? We're shooting tropical fruit colors first. Mango! Key lime! Passion fruit! Let's go." He raised his voice. "Chop-chop!"

They posed in Central Park with the horses, on the ground and in the saddle, for what seemed like the rest of Alexa's life.

"I'm soooo bored!" Charlotte complained.

"Me too," said Gen.

"I still have to pee bad," Mel said, but they were still under orders not to move from the spot.

66 **All I want to do is take off and go for a ride!** *99*

"All I want to do is take off and go for a ride!" Alexa said to Olivia.

"As do I."

Only Kiyoko seemed unsurprised by the interminable slow pace of the shooting. "Miko has told me. Modeling is like a combination of crucifixion and childbirth. Only it takes a little longer and the pay is better."

"Ha!" Olivia brightened. "Can I borrow that? I

hadn't heard that one before."

"Borrow away, Oliver. Just get us the hell out of here soon. I can't take much more of this. My head feels like a fish flopping on a deck."

Olivia looked from Kiyoko to the horse Hal was holding for her. "Can you mount?" she asked.

Kiyoko squinted at her.

"You want to get away. Get on," she said, taking the black horse's lead rope from Hal. "I'll 'pony' you. Lead you."

Kiyoko nodded. "Good. Because I don't know from horses." She put a mango-tinted leather boot in the stirrup and pulled herself into the saddle.

Olivia giggled. "You've led a sheltered life."

"Yeah," said Mel. "You really ought to get out more." She swung up onto her horse in one swoop, like a trick rider.

"Wow!" Alexa said. "I didn't know you could do that!"

"You never asked!"

"What do you say, Gen?" Alexa gave her a glance. "Still want to ride with us?" She was checking Harvard's girth.

Gen hesitated. "I . . . would. But I don't need any grief from Jonah." Alexa couldn't see the expression in her eyes behind the sunglasses. "You all go ahead. Don't worry. I never saw you leave." She looked at Charlotte for support.

Charlotte sighed. "Me neither."

Alexa shrugged and got up on Harvard. Olivia followed. The four girls walked their horses down the path, hearing Jonah's cries get fainter and fainter as they moved away.

"There is just one problem," Alexa said, trotting a bit to catch Kiyoko and Olivia. "We might attract attention from the police."

Kiyoko tossed her hair before remembering that that hurt. "Ow! Yes, I tend to turn heads, but aren't you being a little paranoid?"

Olivia explained. "We're not on the proper bridle path, is all. We'll have to keep an eye open for cops until we get there."

The four *Flirt* interns did indeed attract attention. Dressed alike in buff breeches and white sleeveless shirts, they each wore a different shade of tropical-fruit-colored boots, which, as Jonah had predicted, clashed brightly against the horses' darker coats. They had left their matching tropical-fruit-colored bags back at the trailer with Hal, who said he would watch them.

"Come on, Harvey," Alexa said, urging him to the

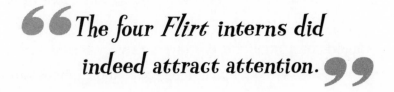

"The four *Flirt* interns did indeed attract attention."

front of the line. "Let's get going. I don't want to give Officer Cage any more reasons to recite the park rules."

After standing around all day, it felt good to be free. Even the horses seemed to think so. They enjoyed a brisk trot down the bridle path, putting distance between themselves and Jonah and the crew. As they skirted the Sheep Meadow that both Alexa and Harvard remembered from their run, Alexa's cell phone rang. She let the others pass her again as she slowed down to answer it.

"Alexa." It was Gen's voice, but it wasn't the usual Gen. "I know you're not going to believe this." There was something different in her tone, something almost . . . convincing.

"So why call me?" Alexa let Harvard walk along behind the group.

"Because you take the pictures."

Alexa let this sink in for a moment.

"Now, I know you can't stand me. And I know maybe I deserve that a little bit. Either way, you shouldn't have posted that picture of Krissa and me. But there's nothing I can do about that now." She paused. "Except tell you the truth."

Oh no! What horrible secret was Genevieve Bishop about to reveal? Now Alexa wasn't sure she wanted complete honesty from her rival.

"That's okay, Gen. I already know about you

planting Madonna's scarf on Ben at the club that night. You don't have to tell me anything else."

"Oh, but I do."

Alexa waited.

"Those first two times I gave you a tip on El Torero? I was making them up. And then the thing with Ben and Jims and Krissa . . . Well, after sitting around feeling sorry for myself for a few days, I realized . . . I owe you. And right now, I swear to god, hope to die, I have an honest-to-gosh, bona fide lead on your man. I'll call you right back when we get an exact location on him."

This was far too easy.

"What do you want in return?"

Gen gave a sad little laugh. "At this point? You can take my picture off your website or not, it doesn't matter."

She hung up.

Who could know if Gen Bishop was telling the truth? No lie detector test in the world would be able to decipher that twisted mind.

"Hey, Alexa!" Mel shouted from up ahead. "The path's over here. Come on!"

Just then, Alexa saw a carriage drawn by a white horse, headed down a paved road toward the zoo, with a passenger in back. It looked like Ben's friend Davey's rig. Could that be Ben? She checked her kiwi-colored watch. The photo session had run long. It was nearly four o'clock. Was it Ben, planning to surprise her?

If so, could she trust him?

She circled Harvard back, to get a better look.

It might be him. Alexa's mind raced, returning to the other night on the boat—before Gen had shown up, before she'd had any reason to doubt Ben's sincerity. The date itself had been magical, the kiss . . . well, that kiss had been like fireworks. That she couldn't deny.

Alexa started to urge Harvard in that direction when her phone rang again. She pulled the horse up short. "Yes?"

"It's him!" Gen said excitedly. "El Torero. Fifth Avenue and Seventy-Ninth. He's getting his shoes shined. From where you are, if you start riding right now, you should be able to catch him. I mean it this time. Now, go!"

The line went dead.

As Alexa watched Ben's carriage slip away, she spotted a lone horse and rider standing at the far end of the meadow. It wasn't one of her group—they had moved on. Was it possible that Alexa's undercover tactics were being used against her? How did Gen know where Alexa was . . . ? Had she followed them on Buttons after all?

Although Alexa had been burned repeatedly by Gen Bishop, the dream of finally bagging El Torero on film came back to haunt her once more, with a vengeance. It

> **"What would she rather have? A picture of a man who would probably never kiss her? Or a kiss from someone who just wouldn't let her take his picture?"**

would be a shame to have come so close only to lose the chance! Gen could be telling the truth this time. Hadn't she said she wanted nothing in return? Hadn't she said the photo on the website was something she deserved?

"Well, didn't she, Harvey?" Alexa asked the horse.

Harvard rolled an eye as if to say, *You can't fool me.*

Alexa sighed heavily. "You understand human nature better than I do, boy!"

Think, chica, think! Alexa chided herself. What would she rather have? A picture of a man who would probably never kiss her? Or a kiss from someone who just wouldn't let her take his picture?

She only had to think about that for a split second. For once, photography was going to have to take a backseat to life. "I need to be following Ben!" she said out loud. She clapped her heels on Harvard's sides and sent him after the carriage.

⌕　⌕　⌕　⌕

Love can do funny things, Alexa thought a few mornings later, on her way up to Josephine Bishop's private office. Despite the threat of demotion, expulsion, and extradition, the *porteña* couldn't muster one speck of doom. Dread at having her work thrown out the window? Being sentenced to peddling subscriptions? Losing her very first job and being sent home? Barely a tremor. There was something about Ben Smith that gave Alexa courage.

> ❝ *Love can do funny things.* ❞

"I am in total, nonrefundable, uncontrollable, indescribable love," she told the elevator computer, after both saying and pressing the first three letters of her last name. She and Ben had spent the past few evenings together, walking around town for hours on end, seeing his favorite places, and finding a few new ones of their own—coffee houses, movie houses, house-houses. But mostly, they had talked—about everything. And knowing how Ben felt about her gave Alexa the boost she needed to carry on. She'd find a way to hang on to the internship . . . somehow.

This time, when she stepped out of the private

elevator, Delia sent her right in. Josephine Bishop looked up from her work. The magazine mogul looked as though she'd had a long day. Was that a crease in her cherry red, satin Anne Klein dress? Was that a crease in her *forehead*? Alexa tried not to stare.

Ms. Bishop motioned Alexa over to her computer monitor.

"Someone kindly forwarded me this link in an e-mail. Is this . . . 'blog' . . . yours?" she asked tiredly, as though knowing the answer. "Never mind. Genevieve says it is, and a simple investigation will confirm it. I cannot express the shock I felt upon recognizing who"—she faltered—"not that it's a complete surprise, granted . . ." She looked her intern frankly in the eye for the first time. "Let's face it, Ms. Veron, there's no denying the veracity of this shot."

"I just happened to be there with my camera," Alexa said quietly.

Bishop held her gaze. "You realize I won't condone such behavior. We'll be calling your parents, obviously." She moved the mouse and displayed Alexa's

> **❝ For the first time since she'd been here—maybe even for the first time in her life—Alexa felt certain she could do this job. ❞**

photo archive. "And the rest of these on the blog? Just as tawdry? Also lucky shots?" She sighed. "We like to think our interns have higher standards than most girls their age, but then they'll turn around and display the most juvenile behavior, like wearing denim to work or unscrewing the lightbulbs in the loft."

Alexa shrugged.

Bishop zoomed in on her "art shots" folder. "What is this?" She silently scrolled through them—the leather jacket and daisies, the ripped stocking, the model's shoe, and Olivia's boot.

Alexa waited.

"Hmmm . . ."

Click!

"Interesting . . ."

Click!

"This is quite energizing . . ."

Bishop buzzed Delia. "Get Lynn Stein up here right away."

And in the time it took to say *"muy de la banana,"* Alexa's prospects had turned inside out. She tried not to think about Ben as the two honchos pored over her work on the blog, exclaiming about raw talent and moldable potential. They called in some of the other editors for their opinions. Responses were positive.

Wow! Alexa thought. Sure, she had run around with a camera for weeks, shooting everything in sight and calling herself an artist. But for the first time since she'd been here—maybe even for the first time in her life—Alexa felt certain she could do this job. That she could really become a good photographer.

After the staff had finally left the office, Josephine Bishop turned to Alexa.

"Ms. Veron. Why didn't you show us these photos before?"

Alexa hesitated. "I . . . didn't think they were fashionable enough."

Bishop scrolled through them again. "This rawness, this realness . . . this is what fashion is." She was silent another moment. "And there's more to them than just that."

She closed the program window and pushed back from her desk. She got up, walked over to the window, and looked out at the cityscape. Alexa held her breath.

Finally, Ms. Bishop turned and faced her. "Well, you've done it, Ms. Veron."

Alexa's heart sank, but then she thought she saw the tiniest glimmer of sincerity, maybe even respect, in her mentor's eye, as opposed to the usual unmitigated scorn.

Bishop rubbed her hands together. "From one professional to another, I have to say, you've wowed me. You've done your job, and you've held up your end of the internship. We'll definitely be using your art photos in the fall issue."

Alexa felt weak from the news. She gathered up her kiwi-colored bag and rose in her kiwi-colored boots, relieved that she had finally succeeded just by putting her skills to use . . . by seeing the world simply and honestly through the camera's eye—the good as well as the evil. As Kiyoko had said, that was what she was all about.

"Just one minute."

Alexa froze.

"Business is business, and I generally don't let personal problems enter into it. But this fiasco with my niece complicates things."

Alexa's heart sank. She had wanted to take it all back, and she knew it was her own fault she'd thought of that too late.

Bishop leaned forward conspiratorially. "You remove Genevieve's unfortunate photos from the Internet, and I'll forget about calling your parents on this issue."

Forget calling her parents? If that happened, then maybe they'd let her come back and visit Ben next year . . . and look at fine arts colleges.

"You mean, I can stay?"

Josephine Bishop regarded Alexa with something that might have been humor. "You can stay. Now . . . Ms. Veron. Is there anything else you want to share with me

66 *Thanks for the opportunity.* **99**

before we close the book on this matter?"

Share? Alexa thought about it. Perhaps it was rule-breaking time now—time to break her own rules. In the spirit of all that had happened, should she make an effort to show more maturity? Should she promise not to wear jeans at the office, to dress more professionally? Should she admit that she was the one who had been unscrewing the lightbulbs in the loft?

"Ms. Bishop, I . . ."

Well? Should she?

"Ms. Bishop . . . I . . . just want to say thanks. Thanks for the opportunity. The horse, the internship . . . all of it."

Bishop nodded and eyed her silently, indicating that the meeting was over.

Alexa left the office and stepped confidently into the elevator, and the door slid shut.